DEAR NEIGHBOUR

no boundary to murder

ANNA WILLETT

Published by

The Book Folks

London, 2020

This book is a work of fiction. Names, characters, businesses, organizations, places and events are either the product of the author's imagination or are used fictitiously. Any resemblance to actual persons, living or dead, events or locales is entirely coincidental. The spelling is British English.

ISBN 978-1-913516-68-0

www.thebookfolks.com

For my daughters

Chapter One

Amy bit into her bun and gave a nod of appreciation, all the while loathing the taste of grease and processed cheese, not to mention the feel of the plastic seat that stuck to the back of her thighs. A short cotton skirt had been a poor choice for a place like Zippy's. Since Zane lost his job, the fast food joint was now as close to a date as they came. Disliking the bitterness of her thoughts almost as much as she despised the burger, she set the sloppy mess on its crinkled wax-paper wrapper and took a sip of cola.

"Did you hear anything about the storeman job?"

She hoped the question had come out as a casual inquiry, but from the way Zane's dark brows tugged together she realised she missed the mark on casual and in his mind she was once again nagging. Now she'd have to deal with his petulance as well as the sour, greasy reflux that inevitably followed their nights out. It was a mean thought, especially when he'd been trying so hard to get a decent job. Was it Zane's fault that A. C. Electrical had to cut back on staff? Was it his fault money was tight? Was he to blame for her crappy life? These were the little questions she asked herself whenever his mood turned dark. Questions that helped keep things in perspective.

"No." He shrugged and grabbed a handful of her fries. "It wasn't the right job for me so it's probably a good thing."

Surprised by his unusual optimism, Amy barely noticed he'd eaten the last of her fries. Optimism was good; something she could work with. Maybe she could even use his upbeat humour to wrangle the conversation her way for once.

"Maddie's parents are letting her use their holiday house next weekend and she asked if we wanted to go down to Bunbury for a couple days?" She waited, watching his face for signs of irritation. "A few couples are going. It'll be a sort of party. Sounds like fun." She could hear a note of pleading in her voice, but couldn't stop herself. "I said I'd ask you."

Zane leaned back, resting his head against the top of the booth. "Is Spider going?"

"Um, maybe. I'll check with Maddie," Amy replied, knowing she'd have to make sure Spider made the invitation list if she wanted Zane to join her that weekend.

Zane used the back of his hand to wipe a shiny layer of grease off his lips. In that second Amy wondered why she put up with all the crappy dates and Zane's sleazy friend, not to mention his mood swings. She wondered why she'd compromised everything she believed in to cover up his mistakes. Mistakes that cost a young man his life and stole a chunk of Amy's soul. The answer was simple and excruciating at the same time: she loved him and had done so for the past year. It wasn't an easy love, not like the ones she'd grown up watching on TV. What she felt for Zane was complicated: a mixture of longing and resentment, of guilt and pain. It was a love that had turned her into a willing criminal.

Zane could be sweet and thoughtful and when he wanted, he could make her feel like the most important woman in the world. Although not so much lately. Not since he'd lost his job and started hanging around people like Edward Crease, or Spider as Edward liked to be called. Having Spider with them on their weekend away would put a damper on the party, but at least Zane would consider the trip.

"It might be okay," Zane said, a smile lifting his full lips into the shape of a red bow. A bow Amy wanted to trace with her fingertips.

* * *

On the drive home, Amy couldn't stop her mind from replaying the way Zane slammed the car door and walked away without inviting her inside his house when she dropped him off. She almost always stayed over after one of their dates, but tonight he'd left her sitting behind the wheel like she was his Uber driver and not his girlfriend.

"Am I his girlfriend?" she asked herself, sniffing back tears.

At twenty-eight, Amy wondered if she was getting too old to play these childish games. Or was she always reading too much into everything Zane said or did? Love hurts. At least that's what her mother always said. But was it supposed to twist her insides out? Was it supposed to change her into someone she barely recognised?

As she drove home, she spotted an Italian restaurant. The place was nothing amazing, just a few outside tables and a flapping red canopy. Inside there were candles and white tablecloths that looked rich and expensive under subtle gold lighting. When the traffic lights changed and she pulled away, she caught a glimpse of a couple sitting near one of the windows. The woman had blonde hair, not dissimilar to Amy's, and was holding a gift wrapped in colourful paper.

It was like viewing another world, one where people weren't scrimping and scrambling for money; a place where things were beautiful and elegant and solid. Without realising it, Amy touched her finger to the birthmark on her temple. A moment later, the restaurant was out of sight and all that remained was a gnawing feeling in the pit of her stomach that was as much yearning as it was sorrow.

Chapter Two

She was keeping count and the last one brought the total to five. Five times Zane had told her to shut up in the hour and forty-five minutes since they had set out for Bunbury. The first few were playful, half-joking jabs, but now his tone was hard and the last one was like a slap in the face.

"I told you I'm not going on some pretentious winery tour." Zane spat the words through clenched teeth. "I agreed to come on this trip to make you happy, so how about thinking about me for once? I don't drink wine and you know I'm broke."

The skin on Amy's fingers burned with the force of gripping the steering wheel. It was better to say nothing when he got this way. It was safer to let the storm pass and wait for the sun to come out, especially since when Zane was happy it felt like the sun shone just for her.

"When we get there," he continued, "I don't want you agreeing to anything. Just..."

Out of the corner of her eye she could see him shaking his head.

"Just think about what I want. Hey." He jabbed a finger into her ribs with enough force to make her jump. "Watch the road. There's the turn."

"Sorry," Amy said, not really sure why she was apologising.

Saying sorry seemed to be her new habit. Sorry Zane. Sorry Mum. Sorry everyone. It was like a nervous tick – something she couldn't control any more than blinking.

"Why is this street called Cobblestone Lane when there are no cobble stones?" Zane asked as they turned onto the narrow stretch of road.

Amy thought of answering, but had no idea why a semi-suburban street built on a grey bitumen road would have such a name. Besides, anything she said would probably only take the shut-up toll to six. With her throat constricting from the effort of holding back tears, one more shut-up might be too much and then she'd be crying. Zane hated it when she cried.

"This place isn't my idea of a holiday," Zane complained, pointing at the short cluster of aging buildings.

A row of scruffy houses facing a stretch of overgrown bushland wasn't what Amy had expected either. In her mind, she pictured a beach shack, shabby chic and overlooking dunes, somewhere they could watch the sunset while sipping ice cold beer, a place where the old Zane might reappear and the nagging guilt might be swallowed by the rush of waves.

Maddie's house was number five in a row of six homes. The squat fibrocement building sat on a sprawling front lawn pockmarked with yellow grass. Amongst the dead sward sat a rusted trampoline. Disappointment and hurt feelings made it painful for Amy to put on a happy face, but somehow she found the will to smile as she turned off the engine.

"Good luck renting this dump." Zane nodded towards the for-lease sign that abutted the mailbox.

Amy chuckled, knowing it was the response he expected, but her attention was on the place next door, the last house on the street before the surrounding bush closed in. A colonial style home with lush gardens, frilly ironwork and a wraparound veranda that sat apart from the other buildings like an aging relic dropped awkwardly on the edge of semi-suburbia.

As they exited the car and walked towards the house, Amy's eyes were drawn to the neighbour's home. Like the Italian restaurant, this particular house, even in its faded grandeur, offered the possibility of something more. Something less shabby and tawdry. Was she wrong to want more?

* * *

"They're okay. Not stuck up or anything. Just..." Maddie raised her shoulders. "Just old, you know?"

Amy nodded and picked up the jug, pouring herself a glass of the fruity concoction Maddie called punch. They were on the back deck half shaded by a resplendent Jacaranda tree in full bloom which made the space much more inviting than the front of the house. With the barbeque sizzling and the smell of sausages and onions filling the yard, Amy felt some of her earlier disappointment ebbing.

"His name's Frank and she's Greta. Frank and Greta… um… Foxhall. My dad says she's loaded – at least her father was loaded. They sold my dad this place about three years ago. I think they own all the houses on this road." Maddie waved a hand in the direction of the neighbour's house. "This street was named after the old lady's father. Something Cobblestone and…" She leaned in and tucked a strand of brown hair behind one ear while her ample breasts rested on the glass table. "They've got no kids or family so my dad reckons everything will go to charity when they fall off the perch."

"That's sad," Amy said glancing at the fence line. "All alone in that big house. It must be hard."

"Life is hard," Joe said behind her as he poked at a sausage. "Look at us. We've got plenty of sausages, but no buns."

"Joe..." Maddie rolled her eyes and tossed a napkin in her boyfriend's direction. "You really are weird."

Amy couldn't help smiling as she watched her two friends' playful interaction. It had been a while since she'd shared anything close to light-heartedness with Zane. Seeing Maddie and Joe together made her wonder if she was hanging onto the idea of something that had never been real. She'd pinned all her hopes on this weekend, praying that miraculously the old Zane would reappear. But what if the old Zane was only an illusion? What if it was only a wisp of happiness that no longer existed?

"Who's weird?"

Zane's voice made Amy flinch. Before she could turn around, he was leaning over her, setting his beer on the table. As Maddie recounted their conversation about the elderly neighbours, Zane let his hands rest on Amy's shoulders. She was wearing a strappy sundress and the feel of his skin against hers set off a tingle that ran the length of her body.

"My dad says the old lady's sitting on a fortune."

Maddie was still talking, but Amy was barely listening. Just being this close to Zane made her momentary doubts about their relationship seem trivial. His hands on her shoulders, the familiarity with which he let his thumb massage the base of her neck took her breath away. It was a connection that was so much stronger than the playful back and forth between Maddie and Joe.

"Spider's here," Zane said, leaning in so his lips were near her ear.

With his breath on her neck, Amy wanted him to kiss her and at the same time she was afraid of how she might react in front of her friends.

"I'm going with him to see a mate," Zane continued. "I'll be back later."

The shock of his words pulled her out of the spell his closeness had cast. Drawing away, she rubbed her hand on the back of her neck trying to erase the heat left by his fingers. Not waiting for her to respond, Zane was already on the move. A second later the back door clattered shut, telling her he'd gone.

It was an awkward moment, one that left her feeling stupidly emotional. They'd only arrived an hour ago and already Zane had something better to do than spend time with her. She was unimportant to him and judging by the way Maddie stood and busied herself with the paper plates and napkins as Joe turned back to the barbeque, they saw it too.

Grateful she didn't have to make eye contact with her friends, Amy picked up her glass and downed the overly sweet punch in two gulps.

"Sorry you've gone to so much effort with the barbeque, but I have a headache so I'm going to have a lie down. Sorry," she blurted again and stood too quickly, bumping the table with her thigh.

"Are you okay?" Maddie asked, grappling with the beer bottle Zane had left next to the punch; trying to stop it from rolling off the table. "I've got some paracetamol in my bag if–"

"No." Amy winced at the shrillness in her voice. "I mean… It's nothing. Just the long drive that's all."

Before she turned and headed for the back door, she caught the look that passed between Maddie and Joe. Was it pity or worry? Maybe a combination of both. Either way, Amy bet they were sorry they'd invited her.

When she reached the bedroom she and Zane would be sharing, she took care to close the door as silently as possible before climbing into one of the two single beds. Pulling the pillow out from under her head, she clasped it to her face. When the tears came, there was no sound.

Chapter Three

Dusty light softened the shabby room and turned the afternoon into evening. The pillow under Amy's cheek, damp with tears, clung to her skin as Zane's voice roused her from a restless slumber.

"Hey, kiddo. Wake-up."

Still fuzzy from sleep, resentment came rushing back. Resentment for the pain he'd put her through and now for the intrusion on her nap. Yet, instead of telling him to leave she forced herself to sit up.

"Sorry about leaving like that but it was important," he continued, his voice soft yet unmistakably excited.

Despite his earlier behaviour she couldn't resist the pull of his good mood. When his silhouette, blurred by shadows, drew closer, she made no move to evade his touch.

"I've got good news," he said, rubbing her bare arm. "Come out to the lounge."

The TV had been turned low, softening the echo of nearby laughter. As they entered the room, Maddie and Joe, half-entangled in each other's arms on the couch, turned her way.

"How are you feeling?" Maddie asked, lifting her head from Joe's shoulder.

Confused for a moment, Amy wondered if the couple had heard her crying. Instinctively, her hand went to her face, touching the puffy skin around her eyes then seeking out the port-wine stain birthmark that marred her left temple.

"Your headache," Maddie prompted. "Is it any better?"

"Yes," Amy said, not meeting her friend's gaze. "Much better. I just needed a nap. Sorry if I made a fuss."

Feeling awkward standing in the middle of the room, she sat in the nearest armchair and turned her attention to the old sitcom playing on TV.

"I got a job," Zane said, sitting on the arm of her chair. "At Markson Electronics as an assistant manager." He slid his arm around her shoulders and pulled her against his chest. "Things are looking up."

She'd been praying for this news for almost three months and now instead of feeling elated she had the sensation she was missing something. It was then she noticed Edward standing in the archway that led to the kitchen. Arm resting on the wall with one hip jutted out, his eyes were on her: a half-smile lifting the corner of his mouth. It was a cruel mouth, thin lipped and wide.

No matter where he was, Edward always found a way to pose. Always leaning dramatically or tipped back in a chair, he somehow managed to arrange himself in a way that was overly relaxed – infinitely confident. And while his body appeared at rest, his eyes were watchful.

"That's wonderful." Amy forced as much enthusiasm as she could muster. "I'm so excited for you," she said, turning her face up to Zane.

To her surprise, he leaned in and kissed her, letting his lips linger against hers. She felt a familiar tingle of pleasure, not just because of the pressure of his mouth on hers, but also because she knew Edward was watching. She wanted him to see that no matter how hard he tried to come between them, it was her Zane wanted. She could give Zane something Edward never could.

When Zane pulled back to continue talking, Amy snatched a glance in Edward's direction and noticed the smile she'd seen only minutes ago had turned into a smirk, a mocking expression that made her shift in her seat. Again, she had the impression she'd stumbled into the middle of a conversation, only understanding half of what was going on.

"Maddie reckons her parents will be okay with us taking this place, so all we have to do is move in," Zane said, spreading his arms wide.

Arms still splayed, he was waiting for her to say something. She opened her mouth to speak, but the words wouldn't come. Was he asking her to move in with him? Living together was something she'd dreamed of, but this wasn't how she'd pictured it. And did he mean for them to live in Bunbury? Two hours away from the city? Two hours away from her mother and little sister?

"You mean live here?" The question came out sounding incredulous. Some of the excitement left Zane's face. "Live in Bunbury?" she tried again, but couldn't hide her disbelief.

"Why not?" Zane asked in a tight voice. "There's a Day Mart here. It's not like you've got a brilliant career going in Perth."

Amy glanced around the room not wanting to have a conversation that would inevitably turn into an argument in front of her friends *or* Edward. Moving in together should have been something they discussed in private, not sprung on her like this. One glance at the hardening expression on her boyfriend's face told her that he wouldn't be put off. If she baulked at the idea, he might never ask again.

"Yes," she said. "I suppose so, but maybe we could find somewhere in Perth first and–"

"Don't you get it?" Zane snapped. "I've got a job here." He jabbed his finger towards the floor. "In the city, the best I can hope for is a job in a fast food joint. Is that what you want for me? A thirty-year-old with a business degree asking kids if they want fries with their burgers?"

"Zane..." Amy hated the begging sound in her voice. "Can we talk about this privately?" She put a hand on his arm, but he was already shrugging her off.

"Forget it." Zane stood and stormed out of the room.

A moment later, the bedroom door slammed and Amy was left staring into Edward's muddy grey eyes.

Chapter Four

With her scant collection of belongings bundled into the back of the car and the blistering heat of the city far behind them, Amy's reservations flew away on the cool breeze wafting through the window. Zane was smiling, singing along with some old pop tune on the radio and she felt herself being swept up in his high spirits. If this move made him happy, maybe it was exactly what they needed.

It was only when they pulled into the driveway of their new home that her resolve wavered. The dying lawn and sagging porch looked more forlorn than she remembered, and the rusted trampoline made her think of a giant mechanical insect: a sinister creature waiting for nightfall to scurry across the lawn on its rusty legs. The idea of living with that thing on the lawn made her want to shiver.

"Here we are," Zane said, turning off the engine.

"There are spokes sticking out of that thing." Amy pointed to the trampoline. "It's dangerous."

"You'll just have to be careful not to run into it in the dark," he said with a laugh.

She knew he was joking, but why did he have to mention the dark? Watching him jump out of the car like he didn't have a care in the world ignited a flicker of resentment and made Amy wonder *why* she was in Bunbury. Why had she left everything behind? Not that she had much to begin with: a nowhere job and a single bed in a room she shared with her twelve-year-old sister. This, she reminded herself, might be the start of a life she and Zane could share. One day they'd look back on the house on Cobblestone Lane and laugh at their humble beginnings.

He had a job now – a good one. She had an interview at the local Day Mart. Everything was going well. It was something to hold onto, only the idea of interviewing for a job, of meeting strangers, and trying to find her place in a new store made her throat tighten with dread.

"Let's go." The thumps of Zane's palms on the bonnet of the car startled her out of her reverie and into action.

Half an hour later, most of their belongings were piled on the lounge room carpet. A modest pile, it seemed, for the contents of two people's lives.

"I left my phone in the car. Run out and grab it for me, babe," Zane said, flopping on the couch.

She thought of telling him to run out and get his own phone, but bit her tongue. He was in a good mood. No. He was in a great mood, happier than she'd seen him in months. Saying the wrong thing could plunge them into an argument and that wasn't how she wanted them to spend their first night living together.

"Okay." Amy paused as she walked by the couch and leaned over him.

"It's going to be okay here, isn't it?" she asked, brushing a lock of dark hair off his forehead.

How she loved his hair with its glossy sheen. She craved the silky feel of it on her neck whenever they made love.

"It's going to be better than okay." Zane dropped his voice to a husky whisper as his hand caressed her thigh. "It'll be full moons and red balloons."

She couldn't help but giggle at his words. Amy loved him like this: playful and intense at the same time. This was the real Zane; the man she'd fallen in love with.

On her way to the car she found herself staring at their neighbour's garden with its colourful assortment of flowers and shrubs. She didn't know a great deal about plants, but enough to recognise petunias, donkey orchids, and stock. How much work, she wondered, would it take to turn their patch of scrub into something as beautiful?

Still thinking about the work and more importantly the cost involved in establishing a garden, she opened the car door and grabbed Zane's phone from the console. About to head back to the house, she glanced at the mobile and noticed Zane had several text messages. While she couldn't see what was in the messages she was able to read Spider's name.

She couldn't say why, but the idea that Edward had so much to say to her boyfriend didn't sit well with her. Spider Crease was bad news. How bad she didn't know and hoped she'd never have to find out. He crept into other people's lives much like an arachnid might spin its web in the corner of a bedroom. That was what Spider was trying to do to them, but she wouldn't let him. She'd make Zane so happy he wouldn't need Edward "Spider" Crease.

She wasn't a snoop, but for a moment she considered punching in Zane's code and reading the messages. Would it be wrong for her to take a quick look? She and Zane were living together now. Didn't that mean they shouldn't have secrets? Still weighing the pros and cons of going through his messages, she looked up and found herself staring at her neighbour.

The old man, bent over some sort of flowering bush, wore a battered straw hat and a blue long-sleeve shirt. Before she could look away, he glanced in her direction. They were at least twenty-five metres apart, but even from a distance and shadowed by the brim of his hat, Amy thought she could see the neighbour's eyes narrow. He straightened and she was struck by the solidness and size of his form. Wide shoulders and thick arms. For a moment, he stood immobile. When he raised a hand in greeting, his movements were surprisingly graceful. Without thinking, she did the same, only realising she was still holding the phone after she'd waved it like a trophy.

Feeling a little ridiculous, she lowered her hand and hurried back into the house. When the front door closed, it dawned on her that her speedy departure might have appeared rude. The old guy was only trying to be friendly and she'd run the other way. With Zane's text messages all but forgotten, she handed him the phone.

"Did you get lost?"

"No." Amy kept her tone light. "Just stopped to take another look at that trampoline."

She wasn't sure why she'd chosen to lie instead of mentioning the old man next door. Nor did she know why she felt relieved when Zane shrugged and turned his attention to the phone. Her gut was telling her to keep the interaction to herself and for now she intended to do just that.

Chapter Five

Zane left early, taking Amy's car and leaving her no choice but to catch a bus. With her interview set for 10:00 a.m., she set out before nine o'clock determined to be on time if not early. Dressed in black pants and a pale blue blouse that tied at the throat with a loose bow, she shifted from her left to right foot as she waited for her ride, all the while regretting her choice of black heels. *Heels.* What was she thinking? She was applying at Day Mart, not Vogue Magazine.

Let people know you mean business. That's what her mother always said. *Put your best foot forward.*

Looking down at the tops of her feet as they turned red in the morning sun, she wondered if taking interview advice from a woman who'd worked as a kitchen hand for the past fifteen years was the wisest choice. *No*, she reminded herself. Her mother was much more than her mundane job. Once a paramedic, Catherine Holt had given up her career for a job that offered child-friendly hours. She'd always put her daughters first and provided as best she could. Just thinking about her family tugged at Amy's heart. It had only been one night and already she missed home.

Forty minutes later and she was seated in the Day Mart manager's office with her feet throbbing and a clipboard balanced on her lap.

"All right." Mr Hodges held his hand out gesturing for her to pass over the application form. "Hm." He tapped a finger to his lips as he read through the paperwork.

As Amy watched the man's eyes travel over the sheet, she couldn't help wondering why she'd had to go through the process of writing out an application when she'd already submitted the form online. Her gaze travelled down and she noticed a scrap of what looked like tissue paper stuck to the skin on his meaty neck. As he read, Amy watched the paper, unable to pull her gaze away.

"I see you've worked on the service desk," Hodges said. He had bulbous eyes that were watery and pale. They reminded Amy of puddles, washed out and tired.

"Yes," she replied, trying to ignore the swatch of tissue paper. "I've had extensive experience with returns and customer service. I also–"

"We can't offer you a position on the service desk," Hodges interrupted. "The best we can do for now is filling shelves. Two shifts a week." As he spoke, the tissue paper travelled up and down.

"Oh, I see." Her hand longed to stray to her temple but instead she folded her arms. "I thought I was applying for a full-time customer service role. When I filled out the application it said–"

"That position has been filled." Hodges tossed her application form on his desk. "It's filling shelves or nothing I'm afraid. At least for now." He shrugged. "Sales are down and the store is struggling to compete with the online market. I'm sorry I can't offer more."

She'd started out filling shelves seven years ago and was painfully aware of how hard it was on the back and shoulders. What's more, two shifts a week would barely cover the rent. After paying a month's rent in advance and an eight-hundred-dollar bond, she had less than three hundred dollars left in her savings account, an amount that wouldn't last long if she had to dip into it for groceries and bills.

She'd shouldered the financial cost of the move, something she had kept from her mother mostly to protect Zane, but also out of shame. Shame that her man couldn't afford the bus fare let alone rent. And then there was that small dark thorn in her side, the one that twisted deeper in the night while a voice in her mind whispered she was being used. A voice that murmured the name Travis, and reminded her of the way his frail body looked when they'd dumped him in a toilet block.

"I know it's not a great start." Mr Hodges leaned his elbows on the desk and fanned out his hands. "But do a good job and stick it out for a while and who knows."

Was it kindness in his voice or condescension? Whatever his tone, the job was still unappealing. Briefly, she wondered what he'd say if she kicked off her shoes and put her throbbing feet up on his desk. Would the swatch of tissue paper come flying off his neck?

If she rejected the job offer, she could get back to the house, pack her things and be ready to leave when Zane brought the car home. With any luck she'd still be able to get her old job back. A job that wasn't fabulous or exciting but was steady work with people she knew and liked: people who accepted her as she was.

"When do I start?" she asked, hoping her smile looked genuine.

* * *

She couldn't quite bring herself to think of Cobblestone Lane as home, but after missing her stop and having walked for half an hour, Amy *was* pleased to see the forlorn house with its pockmarked lawn. With her blouse – the one she thought of as her best – sticking to her back and her blonde hair hanging in sweaty clumps around her cheeks, she stepped onto the porch.

It was then she noticed the little posy of flowers. For a second, she was sure that in her exhausted state she'd stumbled up to the wrong house. One glance over her shoulder at the rusty trampoline confirmed she was indeed at the right place.

The flowers were tied with violet ribbon, the bow looped and narrow. A sheet of paper peeked out from beneath the stems. As she bent to retrieve the gift, she caught the scent of freesia.

She held the flowers close to her chest, enjoying the coolness of the stalks against her palm. She'd never received flowers before, not from Zane or any of her previous boyfriends, if the sad collection of disasters could even be called boyfriends. Once, her little sister Darla had picked daisies and wrapped them in brown paper before presenting them to Amy on her birthday. Holding the flowers and the note made her think of her sister and of the cakes her mother would bake on special occasions.

Half expecting the note to be for someone else, she unlocked the front door and stepped into the gloom of the hallway before she read it.

> *Dear Neighbour,*
> *Welcome to Cobblestone Lane!*
> *We hope these flowers will brighten your new home.*
> *Best wishes*
> *Frank and Greta Foxhall (Number 6)*

The handwriting was sloping and old-fashioned with its swirls and dips. A few short lines, but the unexpected kindness was enough to take the sting out of her disappointing job interview. Maybe this *was* the start of a new life. A happy existence with friendly neighbours. Civilised people who grew flowers and welcomed newcomers.

Was a fresh start possible? She wanted it to be so. Yet, no matter what she did, the craving remained: a craving for a flawless life not marked by her imperfections both external and internal. Could she block out the past? Could she make things beautiful like the candle-lit restaurant?

Kicking off her shoes, she set about putting the flowers in water. The closest thing she could find to a vase was a tall drinking glass, so she set it in the centre of the kitchen table. When she was satisfied with the centrepiece she had arranged, she tied the purple ribbon around the glass. Humming now, she grabbed her phone out of her bag and looked up a recipe.

Three hours later, after a long walk to the nearest grocery store and two calls to her mother, she pulled a hot tray out of the oven. The scones weren't perfect, a little sunken, but not bad for a first attempt. Only sorry she hadn't thought to buy jam and cream, she arranged the scones on a plate. As a final touch she grabbed a flower out of the arrangement and placed it on the side of the plate. Scones in hand, Amy approached Number 6.

"Hello, I'm Amy. I live next door." She tried the words, muttering them so no one would hear her talking to herself. "I'm your neighbour, Amy. Thanks for the flowers." *I sound like an idiot.* "Nice to meet you. I'm Amy."

Turning up on her neighbour's doorstep with baked goods felt like a bright idea a few hours ago, but now in the shadow of the grand home uncertainty rolled in her stomach like a bowling ball. The Foxhalls were older and wealthy, probably cultured and well-travelled. What would they think of her in her worn summer dress and scuffed tennis shoes?

A few steps away from the house she hesitated. It seemed the garden with its sweet-smelling blooms had grown larger, encompassing her and blocking out all glimpses of the sad looking house she'd just left. What was she doing? Meeting new people terrified her and yet here she was holding a plate of over-cooked scones.

Certain she'd made a dreadful mistake and that she'd overestimated the Foxhalls' kind gesture as something more, she turned back towards the road, ready to break into a run. But there were so many windows, the old man or woman might have seen her approaching. She couldn't just run away. Not again. And then there was the note. The neighbours had initiated friendship. No response would be rude.

She was almost at their door. The best thing to do would be to just leave the plate. It would be cute really, an exchange of presents without ever meeting. Running a hand over her hair, she stepped onto the veranda. It was cooler out of the sun. The long expanse of the porch dampened the heat by at least five degrees and went some way to calming her racing pulse. At the foot of the entrance was a weathered doormat, the ideal place to leave her gift.

"Stop!"

The suddenness and urgency of the command took Amy by surprise. Arms outstretched ready to place the gift on the mat, she straightened as if caught committing a crime. Absurdly, she let out a yelp of fear.

In the seconds it took to realise the disembodied voice had come from inside the house, she also heard a thud. Something rattled closer to the door. Just as she tried to take a step back, the door flew open and a figure dressed in white lurched toward her.

Their bodies collided. The impact threw Amy off balance and knocked the plate out of her hands. As the china shattered and shards flew around her feet, Amy found herself confronted by a wild-eyed woman whose face was haloed by a shock of white hair. Amy was briefly aware of something stinging her calf.

"I've got to open the top gate. The horses can't get out." The old woman gripped Amy's upper arms with surprising strength. "They'll burn. They'll all burn," she shrilled, her huge eyes threatening to bulge out of their sockets.

With the woman's fingers drilling into her skin, Amy tried to pull away but couldn't disentangle herself from the woman's manic embrace. Driven by panic and equal measures of embarrassment, Amy put her hand on the woman's chest meaning to push her away, but when she felt the sharp bones beneath her fingers and the heat of the woman's skin, Amy snatched her hand back in disgust.

A man appeared and grabbed the woman's shoulders. "It's okay, love. I opened the gate." His tone was gentle, soothing and coaxing at the same time.

As if entranced by his voice, the woman let go of Amy's arms. "Are they safe?" the woman asked, turning to the man Amy now recognised as the person that had waved to her on the day she and Zane had moved in.

"They're safe," the man answered, running a hand over the woman's wild hair. "Come inside, darling. I'll make us some tea."

As the couple moved back into the house, the man glanced over his shoulder to where Amy stood surrounded by broken china and mushed scones.

"I'm sorry," Amy said, not sure what she was apologising for.

"It's not a good time."

The man's voice had morphed into a deep growl.

"Sorry. Sorry." Amy said, moving back still babbling apologies when the door slammed closed.

In her haste to escape, she missed the second step coming off the veranda and stumbled into an awkward half-fall. Heart thudding, she kept going, exploding into a run that took her through the garden and all the way back to her front door.

She was breathing heavily from the exertion and the need to get inside, desperate to put dense wood and a solid lock between herself and the horrendous spectacle. But when she grasped the handle, the door wouldn't budge. Crying now, Amy rattled the knob. This couldn't be happening. In her haste to meet the neighbours she'd forgotten to turn the latch and now was locked out.

Out of frustration and wretchedness, she kicked the door then gasped at the jab of pain in her big toe. For a run-down holiday house, the door was certainly solid.

Turning back to the street and the dense bush on the other side of the road, she sniffed back tears and considered her options. *Ask a neighbour for help*? The idea was almost laughable. She couldn't go back to the Foxhalls' house and the house on the other side sat vacant. She could wait for Zane to get home. The problem was she had no idea when he finished work because he hadn't bothered to tell her.

Standing on the sagging porch with tears dripping down her face and a trickle of blood staining her calf, she felt a flash of resentment. Zane had forced her to move to Bunbury. He'd forced her to do things she couldn't bear to think about. He'd taken her car without asking and now she was stranded. No. She wasn't just stranded; she'd made a fool of herself and was locked out the house on a stinking hot day.

Pressing her palms into her eyes, she crouched down and then flopped into a sitting position on the sagging porch. What she wanted was the safety of home and her mother's calm reassurance that everything would be okay. Catherine Holt always knew what to do. She'd have a plan of action, striding around the building looking for a way in, not sitting on the porch trying not to have a full-blown melt down.

Amy uncovered her eyes and for a second spots of light danced over her retinas. There was no extraction fan in the bathroom so after her shower that morning she'd opened the window to let the steam waft out. It was a small opening, but one she was certain she could wriggle through.

"All right then," Amy said, dipping her face so she could wipe the tears away with the hem of her sundress.

Chapter Six

"Something smells good."

"It's just toasted sandwiches." Amy spoke over her shoulder, shoving a plate into the microwave, only half-listening as Zane moved around the kitchen.

It was late; almost 7:30 p.m. He worked a long day, but for once her thoughts weren't on Zane and what his mood might dictate. Nor was she hurt that he hadn't called to tell her what time he'd be home. Instead, the scene from the neighbour's veranda replayed in her mind.

The old woman was unwell, confused. It must have been the man who'd left the flowers and note. But why would he invite attention from his neighbour if he was struggling to manage his wife's illness? More importantly, why did Amy care? The encounter had been a disaster. An embarrassing ordeal that made her cringe every time she thought about it. *Stop going over it.*

"What happened to your leg?" Zane asked. He was seated at the table, munching on the toasties. At some point he must have grabbed the plate out of the microwave, but she had been too lost in thought to notice. "Where'd the flowers come from?" he asked, moving on without giving her time to tell him about her leg.

She couldn't say why, but her first impulse was to lie, to make up a story where she didn't look like a needy fool, but what was the point? Zane knew all too well how needy she could be. Hadn't he told her so on countless occasions?

Amy sat opposite him. "I met the neighbours today," she began, enjoying the way his eyebrows rose with attentiveness. "It was kind of embarrassing."

When she'd finished the story, Zane reached across the table and took her hand. "You're sweet," he said and kissed her knuckles.

It wasn't the reaction she expected. Part of her thought he'd laugh, maybe even tease her about how stupid she must have looked. But there was genuine kindness in his voice and after the day she'd had tears pricked her eyes. Tears because she was homesick and also because she'd thought the worst of the man she was supposed to love.

"Come here, kiddo." Zane pushed his plate aside and held his arms wide.

A moment later, Amy was on his lap, her head nestled into his shoulder while he stroked her hair. She loved it when he called her kiddo. The pet name was so simple yet felt more intimate than sex. It was part of their secret bond, a connection the rest of the world couldn't touch.

"You did a nice thing," Zane said, kissing the top of her head. "Give them a day or two and then try again."

Amy pulled back and stared into his eyes – eyes that were dark and unfathomable. Telling her to try again was an odd response, especially for a man like Zane. *A man like Zane.* Before she could wonder what that even meant he manoeuvred her off his lap so he could stand.

"I need a pee." He spoke over his shoulder as he headed for the bathroom.

Amy thought of following and asking why he'd told her to try again. Why a man, who was usually so dismissive of the niceties of life, would advise her to try to make new friends on the street where they lived? But she didn't follow Zane. She picked up his plate and took it to the sink to wash it.

From her position at the draining board she could see the back yard. The Jacaranda in full bloom was pretty by day, but painted silver by moonlight it looked glorious. Maybe Zane was right and she should try again with the Foxhalls. If the wife was unwell, reaching out to them was the neighbourly thing to do. Maybe she could help.

* * *

As it turned out, it wasn't Amy who tried again. At nine o'clock the following morning she opened the door to find Frank Foxhall standing on the sagging porch.

"I wanted to explain what happened yesterday." The old man nodded towards his house. "I want to explain about Greta."

Meeting new people usually made Amy's hands shake and her words catch in her throat and, after their horrendous first encounter, seeing the man again should have turned her into a stuttering mess. Yet, there was something about Frank Foxhall that had the opposite effect on her. A calm fatherly quality that reminded her of the old movies she'd watched with her mother and sister.

"Would you like to come in?" Amy asked, holding the door open.

Ten minutes later, they were seated at the kitchen table facing each other over cups of instant coffee.

"Greta isn't always like that," Frank said, making no move to touch his cup. "She's not like that at all really. She wasn't herself when you saw her."

His size and sadness filled the kitchen; his sorrow an almost tangible thing that Amy could see as clearly as the steam rising off the coffee cups. Emotion was in the timbre of his words and the slump of his broad shoulders. It was etched into the creases of his tanned face. She thought of how upset she'd been the day before and her cheeks flushed with shame. He was struggling and so was his wife. That should have been obvious, but all Amy had thought about was her own embarrassment. She'd never stopped to consider how distressing the encounter might have been for the Foxhalls.

"Please, you don't have to explain." She thought of patting his hand, but was afraid the gesture might be overly familiar.

"I do," Frank said. "I need to explain for my Greta." He held her gaze and the gravity of his intention was there in his eyes. Eyes that were unusual in colour and appearance: dark blue and rimmed with thick black lashes.

"She has Alzheimer's." His voice wavered on the last word. "It's very early stages. She's just a little forgetful, loses her train of thought, but nothing serious. Not…" He paused and drew breath. "Not yet."

He pinched the bridge of his nose. It was a tired gesture, one of a man with the world on his shoulders. A load Amy suddenly wished she could lighten.

"Yesterday was a bad spell," he continued. "The worst so far. You see, she has a urinary tract infection and the doctor tells me it leads to confusion. But she's on the mend and she's much brighter today."

"That's good. I mean that she's brighter," Amy said, trying to put as much positivity into the response as she could.

"Yes." He gave a nod. "Greta, the real Greta… well, she's exceptional. Exceptionally kind." He spread his hands wide and suddenly looked younger than he had on that first day when he'd waved to her. "Exceptionally brave and gracious. Not at all as she appeared yesterday. That's why I wanted to explain and invite you over for afternoon tea." He gave her a smile and the word "dazzling" popped into Amy's head. "Consider it an apology for the way I growled at you."

He was waiting for her to respond. A polite refusal seemed like the safest option and the surest way of avoiding another awful scene. Yet, Amy realised she didn't feel in the slightest bit fearful of meeting Greta Foxhall or venturing back to her neighbour's house.

"I'd like that," she said and felt a flicker of excitement.

Chapter Seven

Cool air fluttering through lace curtains carried a hint of apricot and something floral while outside the sitting room window birds twittered. It was difficult to believe that this ideal setting existed only metres from the ramshackle house with the rusty trampoline garden ornament.

"These are delicious," Amy said, biting into a wafer-thin lemon biscuit.

"Thank you." Greta placed an almost translucent china teacup back on its saucer. "You must take some home with you and have them after dinner."

Amy shook her head. "I couldn't. What about you and Frank?"

Greta turned her head and smiled at her husband. Amy thought she saw something pass between them: an understanding conveyed just by locking eyes. Her suspicions were confirmed when a second later Frank stood and excused himself.

"Sorry," Greta said, smoothing her lilac-coloured skirt. "That was a bit obvious, wasn't it?"

"No," Amy started, but when she saw the glint of amusement in the woman's green eyes she couldn't help but laugh. "Yes, it was a bit."

Greta chuckled. "That man of mine is a dear, but sometimes a girl craves the company of women. And a little gossip." Greta picked up her cup. "Now, Frank tells me you and your fella moved in last Saturday and I see by your lack of ring" – she nodded to Amy's left hand – "you two are not married. So is this your first week living together?"

While the question was a bit probing, Greta's mischievous smile was hard to resist.

"Yes," Amy answered quickly before she had time to fret over how much she should reveal. "It's my first time living with anyone. I mean with anyone that's not family. Zane… He's my first real boyfriend."

She hesitated, searching Greta's face for signs of judgment. Amy was twenty-eight, obviously too old to only have had one real boyfriend. She wouldn't have blamed Greta if she was shocked by the admission, but her neighbour's face with its high cheekbones and perfectly arched brows remained open and interested. So much so that Amy continued to talk, telling Greta more about her relationship than she'd shared with anyone, even her mother.

"Hm." Greta propped her elbow on the arm of the chair and let her chin rest in her palm. "Men can be complex. Some more so than others. But you're obviously in love, so allowances must be made."

"Allowances?" Amy thought it was a strange choice of word.

When Greta answered, her voice was soft, almost dreamy. "Allowances are what we make for love's sake, aren't they?"

"I suppose so," Amy said, noticing the way Greta's eyes were shining with what looked like unshed tears.

Amy wondered what Greta would think of her if she knew what she'd done for love – the sort of *allowances* she'd made.

"If you love someone hard enough," Greta continued, "things have a habit of dropping away. There's no right or wrong, just need."

Amy wasn't sure how to respond or if a response was warranted. An image of Greta, wild-eyed and panicked flashed in her mind making her wonder if the old lady was about to grab her again and start shrieking about horses. At the same time it occurred to her that Frank probably shouldn't have gone off and left her with his wife if she was unstable. Unstable was a harsh word. Greta was unwell, not a lunatic. Not someone to be feared.

Sitting opposite the impeccably dressed woman with her soft white hair arranged into a thick plait that hung over her shoulder, it was almost impossible to reconcile her with the dishevelled creature Amy had collided with on the porch. Still, Amy glanced towards the window hoping to catch a glimpse of Frank in the garden, but saw only blue sky and purple agapanthus. When she looked back, the old lady was pouring tea into her cup.

"Forgive me. I'm a bit of a romantic." Greta blinked and the tears Amy thought she'd seen had vanished. "More tea?"

They talked for almost an hour before Amy, worried she'd tired Greta or had overstayed her welcome, said she had better be on her way.

"Of course, dear. I've probably talked your ears numb," Greta said, rising from the armchair. "But I haven't forgotten I promised you lemon biscuits to take home to your man."

As Amy followed Greta along the hallway, they passed several rooms. One of them contained a black grand piano adorned with an array of photographs in silver frames. What, she wondered, would it feel like to run her fingers over the dark shiny wood.

"Do you play?" Greta asked, stopping their short walk back to the kitchen.

Suddenly aware that she'd been caught staring into the room, Amy flushed with embarrassment. "No. Well, just *Hot Cross Buns* and *Three Blind Mice*. And that was years ago on an electric keyboard. Not that you could call it playing." She put a hand to her temple and pulled a strand of hair forward so that it covered her birthmark. "Sorry. I didn't mean to stare. I've just never seen a piano like that up close."

"Apologies are unnecessary." Greta laid her hand on Amy's arm. "We're neighbours and I hope friends too. So if you'd like to learn, I'd be happy to teach you."

Amy snatched another glance at the piano, imagining herself seated on the padded, velvet stool. "That's kind of you, but I couldn't take up your time."

"It would be to my benefit," Greta said, following Amy's gaze towards the piano. "These sorts of things keep the mind sharp."

"All right." Amy nodded, trying not to grin like an idiot. "I mean yes, please. I'd love to learn."

"Wonderful." Greta let go of Amy's arm and clapped her hands together. "We'll start tomorrow. That will give me time to find the perfect piece."

Amy felt a rush of pleasure. Greta's enthusiasm was contagious, but it was more than that. The idea of learning to play on an elegant grand piano was a dream come true and so was spending time with someone as cultured and kind as Greta.

On her walk home, Amy held the tub of biscuits to her chest. Maybe being away from home was doing her good because in Perth she would have never had the nerve to talk to people like Greta and Frank.

Chapter Eight

"How did it go?" Frank sat down beside Greta on the drawing room floor wincing at the way his kneecaps protested.

"She's perfect." Greta spoke without looking up from the stack of music. "You were right."

He thought he caught a hint of recrimination in her voice, so he put his hand on her shoulder, gently turning her to face him.

"I know it's hard, but you need someone here with you while I tidy up the loose ends. And there's the other thing too." He waited, but she made no response. "You like her, don't you? She seemed pleasant enough."

Greta let out a long breath before answering. "Yes, I like her. She's just the right mix of shy and needy. It couldn't have worked out better if you'd picked her out of a catalogue."

"This isn't the way I wanted things to go. If there was any other way, I'd take it." Frank watched her, trying not to notice the tremble in her once steady hands. "We got lucky with her moving in next door. You see that, don't you?"

When Greta met his gaze, her green eyes were weary. "We could sell number four. I don't want you to have to–"

"No." He saw her flinch and immediately regretted raising his voice. "Sorry, love, but that's out of the question. You're going to need that money. Now, come on," he said, pushing himself off the floor. "My bones are too old for sitting on the rug like a hippie."

To his relief, Greta smiled and held out a hand so he could help her up. Once they were both standing, he pulled her into his arms then leaned down and buried his face in her neck.

"It'll be all right. I promise," he whispered, knowing these were the words she wanted to hear. "Once it's done, everything will go back to normal. We're not going to hurt the girl and by the looks of her, she could use a friend."

"Yes, I suppose so." Greta sounded more relaxed. "When will you do it?"

They were swaying slightly. It felt like they were dancing just as they'd done on warm summer nights before old age and past sins had caught up with them.

"I have the money ready," Frank replied. "I'll take it with me for appearances' sake. Now, we wait for his call."

Greta murmured something he didn't quite catch. Frank closed his eyes noting how frail her body now seemed. He was losing her. Losing her rapidly. Who they were together was ebbing away. Knowing what precious time they had left was being stolen made him want to lash out, but he forced his muscles to relax. He didn't have much left to give, but he would give it all for her.

Chapter Nine

"You'll never guess where I've been." Amy used her elbow to close the front door behind her.

It was early, only four o'clock, but her car was in the driveway so that meant Zane was home. He'd be pleased that she'd made the effort and went back to the Foxhalls' house. She was still a bit puzzled by his enthusiasm when it came to her befriending the neighbours, but what did it matter as long as he was supporting her, encouraging her to spread her wings and be more confident? Wasn't that what they were supposed to do for each other?

The lounge room was empty, but Zane's jacket was draped over the armchair. From the kitchen came a sound resembling a chair scraping the floor.

"I have something yummy for–" She spotted Edward shirtless and with his back propped against the doorframe between the kitchen and laundry. Her remaining words died on her lips.

"I asked Spider to take a look at the washing machine." Zane was at the kitchen sink with his back to her.

She had the sense she'd interrupted something, but wasn't sure what. Had they been talking about her? Would Zane discuss their relationship with Edward? No, she wouldn't believe that. Yet suddenly she felt like an intruder in her own home.

Determined not to be intimidated, Amy set the tub of biscuits on the table. "Hi." She forced herself to look at Edward, hating the sight of his naked torso and the blue and black tattoo swirls that covered his skin.

"I said he could crash here tonight." Zane had a glass now and was running the tap, still not looking at her.

Apart from the sound of the water, the kitchen sat silent. She knew she should say something, but all she wanted was to get away from the smell of Edward's sweat, a heavy musky odour that came off him in waves and made her want to gag.

"You okay with that, Amy?" Edward drew out the *Y* on the end of her name making the question sound mocking and like baby talk. "I wouldn't want to put you out."

"Yes, it's fine." She tried to make her voice cutting, but the words came out sounding feeble and mumbled.

"Hey." Zane was looking at her now, his eyes searching her face with what looked like concern. "What were you going to tell me?" he asked reaching for her hand.

She could feel Edward's eyes on her at the same time Zane's hand closed around her wrist. His touch was usually welcome, but his clammy fingers made her want to shrink from him.

"It's nothing," she said, pulling out of his grasp. "I'll tell you later."

Once out of the kitchen she headed for the bathroom craving a shower with water hot enough to wash away the stink of Spider's sweat. Before closing the door, Amy heard Zane's voice low and muffled, then a peel of laughter that was unmistakably Edward's.

Not wanting to hear more, she closed and locked the door then flipped the lid down and sat on the toilet. With her head in her hands, Amy closed her eyes. Why were they doing this to her? Why was *Zane* doing this to her?

Surely he knew she didn't like Edward and surely Edward's contempt toward her was so clear that even a blind man could see it.

If she wasn't such a coward, she'd go back out there and tell Edward to leave. *I'm sorry, but you can't stay here.* That's what she should have said. Or, better still, forget the apology. *You can't stay here, not tonight or any other night.*

Amy rubbed a finger to the birthmark on her temple. She wasn't brave and that was the problem. She wasn't confident. She was still Splat. Cringing and frightened Splat. Just thinking about the cruel high school nickname made her skin burn with humiliation. She could still hear the shouts that followed her as she scurried off the school bus.

'Hey, Splat. Let me rub that thing for luck.'

'She's got those splat marks all over her, like someone went after her with a paintball gun.'

Her lips and chin trembled as she struggled to push the hurt away. It didn't matter how much time passed or where she went, Amy would always be an outsider. She'd always be Splat.

* * *

She waited until the sound of their voices faded and the car drove away before springing out of bed and getting dressed. She'd be late for work and on her first day, all because she was too weak to stand up for herself in her own house.

Running a comb through her hair and rushing out of the house without breakfast, she jogged the length of Cobblestone Lane, turning the corner in time to see her bus pulling away from the curb. It was 8:30 a.m. and already the sun was strong enough to turn the sweat on the back of her neck into warm trickles that dampened the collar of her new uniform.

Letting out a defeated breath, she shuffled the last few metres and flopped down onto the bus stop bench. She didn't care much about the job. Stacking shelves wasn't exactly her dream career so losing it was no big deal, but the idea of arriving late and being pulled into Mr Hodges' office for a stern talking to was more than she could face. And she needed the money. It was always about the money. What must it be like to be above the daily grind?

"Want a ride?"

She'd been so lost in self-misery she hadn't noticed the rumble of the old blue Mazda's engine as it pulled up to the curb.

Still startled by her neighbour's sudden appearance, it took Amy a second to formulate a response. "Mr Foxhall! Hi."

"It's Frank, remember."

A moment later, Amy settled back in the passenger seat, relieved she'd be avoiding a reprimand on her first day.

"I saw a car parked in your driveway. Is it yours?" he asked with his hands resting on the steering wheel and making no move to drive.

"Yes," Amy answered, wondering if it might not have been better to wait for the bus. "But Zane needs it for work."

"And you catch the bus?" Frank made the question sound like an observation.

"It's not far. I mean it's really no big deal."

Frank's eyes narrowed, but he didn't respond. Amy shifted in her seat wondering how the situation must look, her catching the bus while Zane drove to work.

"It's just until we get on our feet," she added. "Just until we sort things out."

The truth was she didn't know why her boyfriend thought it was okay to take her car without asking or what exactly they were sorting out. But Frank seemed satisfied with the answer.

"Well," he said, checking his mirrors and pulling away from the bus stop. "I'm often going your way so we may as well carpool."

And just like that, the lifts to work became a regular thing. And, after the slightly awkward questions were put to bed, Amy enjoyed Frank's calm and easy company. Just as she came to relish the time she spent with Greta. As the weeks passed, the elderly couple became her reprieve from Spider's growing presence.

Chapter Ten

The piano keys felt familiar, cool and welcoming. The music, a piece called *Fallen Angel*, had at first been challenging and clunky but now flowed as Amy's fingers found the correct keys and rhythm.

"You have a natural aptitude," Greta said, turning the sheet music over. "My old music teacher called it magic fingers."

This was their sixth lesson, something that had become a twice weekly routine. These sessions were now the high point of Amy's week and Frank's and Greta's house an island where she could escape Spider's watchful gaze. A place where she didn't have to worry about her boyfriend's growing disinterest or how lonely her life was becoming. In the Foxhalls' house she pretended she was a different person. A better person.

"Magic fingers." Amy repeated the words enjoying the way they rolled off her tongue. "Huh, I never thought of myself as having magic anything."

"Amy…" Greta's voice was soft. "Don't you know how much you have to offer? Don't you see how special and wonderful you are?"

Amy pulled her hands off the piano keys and dropped them in her lap. "I wasn't trying to fish for–"

"I know." Greta sounded almost angry now. "And I see that birthmark that you're always trying to hide. It doesn't make you any less talented or intelligent or" – she waved a hand in the air – "or any less beautiful."

They were seated next to each other, Amy on the velvet stool and Greta on a kitchen chair. The words coming out of Greta's mouth were like bullets, hitting Amy in the gut. She clenched her hands together wishing the older woman would stop. Just hearing her mention the birthmark made Amy's skin crawl with embarrassment.

"Please, stop." Amy started to stand, but Greta grabbed her wrist.

Greta's usually warm voice was tight with determination. "No. You're going to look at me and hear what I have to say." She softened her tone. "Please."

Amy let herself be pulled down onto the stool, but still couldn't bring herself to look Greta in the eyes.

"We're friends, Amy, and that's why I have to be honest with you." Greta sounded more like herself, now only slightly breathless. "You know I'm sick."

Amy looked up and into Greta's eyes, surprised at the frankness of her question and at the same time unsure how to answer.

"It's all right," Greta continued. "I know Frank told you I have Alzheimer's disease. But *I'm* not the disease if that makes sense."

Amy knew where Greta was going because she'd had the same sort of pep-talks from her mother on countless occasions. Talks meant to help but when coming from attractive people like her mother and Greta, people whose appearance was close to perfect, the words only made Amy feel freakish and awkward.

"Yes. Yes, yes. I understand." Amy nodded, wanting the conversation to end, but sensing Greta had more to say.

"You want me to stop talking about it, don't you?" Greta asked, but didn't wait for an answer. "And I will stop, but first let me ask you, have you ever heard of port-wine stains being called firemarks?"

"Yes, maybe. I'm not sure," Amy replied, trying to keep her lips from trembling. "I've heard just about every name people have come up with for what I've got." *Splat,* she thought, but didn't say.

She'd only ever said the name out loud once. Lying in Zane's arms with the darkness covering her shame, she told him about the nickname. Amy wasn't sure why she'd confided in him. Probably because she'd been carrying the pain of it for so long, she hoped telling the man she loved would take away the word's power over her. She'd wanted him to tell her she was beautiful and the bullies were hateful, but he'd just sniffed and kissed the top of her head. In that moment, she wished she could take the word back because now she feared he would think that humiliating name every time he looked at her.

"Well, I have a firemark of my own," Greta said and raised the hem of her skirt.

Amy's mouth stopped trembling and fell open slightly as her eyes travelled over the burns on Greta's right leg. Skin that appeared melted formed lumpy masses around her knee then stretched out into what looked like scales on her thigh. Even to Amy's untrained eye, the scars seemed old, thickened and edged with ridges.

"It was a bushfire, a bad one. Not far from where we're sitting now. Believe it or not, part of that bushland across the road used to be a paddock. I was trying to open the gate at the top end so the horses could escape the flames and in the process I was burned."

"Greta, I'm sorry. I didn't know." Amy was crying now, not because she was embarrassed, but for the pain and suffering Greta had obviously endured.

"No need to apologise," Greta said flipping down her skirt. "It was a long time ago, almost fifty years. The scars have become a part of who I am. They're my history. My story and, in a strange way they have their own beauty." She patted Amy's hand. "So does your firemark. Don't let anyone make you ashamed of who you are. Don't be ashamed, Amy."

"The music has stopped so I'm guessing you ladies want lunch?" Frank's voice from the kitchen was jovial, breaking through the emotion of Greta's words.

"Thank you, darling. That would be lovely," Greta called with her gaze still fixed on Amy. "Amy, why don't you go upstairs and wash your face? The bathroom is on the right."

Before Amy stood, Greta gave her hand another squeeze and smiled, making the skin at the corners of her eyes crinkle in a way that reminded Amy of a bird's wing, delicate and fragile. There was no trace of confusion in the woman's face, only warmth.

A faint scent of lemon and wood polish permeated the upstairs of the Foxhalls' home as the boards under Amy's shoes creaked. In the bathroom she splashed cold water on her face then patted her skin dry on a thick white towel. Before leaving she took a second to examine the birthmark on her temple.

She always hated the term port-wine stain. In many ways, it was as bad as being called Splat. Both suggested something had been thrown in her face.

"Firemark." She said the word aloud testing the way it felt on her lips.

Her birthmark seemed so small and inconsequential when compared to Greta's burns. So much of Amy's life had been spent fretting over the imperfection when a woman like Greta viewed her scars as part of the beauty of a life fully lived. Could she ever see her own birthmark in the same light, Amy wondered. Could she ever view her birthmark as part of the beauty of a life well lived?

When she'd been rushing upstairs to wash her face, she hadn't taken in much of her surroundings, but on her way back along the landing she noticed a bedroom door sat open. Below, she heard the clatter of plates and the rush of running water.

She had only intended to stand in the doorway and take a peek at the room that represented another part of the Foxhalls' lives. The room sat as she'd imagined: old-fashioned and elegant. A large brass-framed bed covered in a maroon and pink patchwork quilt sat on top of a large and faded Turkish rug. More lacy curtains covered the two windows, letting in afternoon sunlight that threw intricate golden patterns on the shiny hardwood floor.

A silky-looking green scarf was draped over a cheval mirror. Next to the bed, on either side, sat dark wood nightstands. Amy wondered which side of the bed belonged to Greta. She noticed a book on the nightstand on the right, closest to the window.

Without thinking, Amy entered the room and picked up the book *Love in the Time of Cholera*. The author's name was Spanish. A red rose in bloom adorned the cover. She could imagine Greta sitting in bed reading while Frank dozed beside her. It was a nice image, one that made Amy smile. She made a mental note to see if she could track down a copy of the book. Maybe she'd even join the library. *If I ever get my car back.*

Sounds drifted up from below. The clink of china and mellow voices pulled her out of her daydream. Frank and Greta would be wondering where she was and the last thing she wanted was to be caught snooping.

In her haste to exit the room, Amy's toe clipped the edge of something under the bed, sending the object sliding sideways and revealing a grey bag. Not wanting to leave any trace of her presence in the room, she ducked and grabbed the bag meaning to shove it back under the bed.

The carry-all was canvas, coarse and sturdy. More like something a tradesman would use than anything she imagined Greta or Frank carrying. Frowning, she gripped the bag's edges and felt the weight of something inside.

"What am I doing? What am I doing?" She mumbled the words knowing full well what she was doing. More snooping.

Peeling back the zip revealed a draw-string pouch similar to the book-bag she'd carted back and forth to the library when she was in primary school, only unlike her colourful library bag, the pouch was made of raw cotton. Before pulling the bag open, Amy glanced up. From where she was crouched, she could see over the bed and out onto the landing. There was no one in sight and pausing for a moment to listen told her Frank and Greta were still in the kitchen.

Amy wasn't quite sure what she expected to find. Jewellery? Passports? Instead, the pouch contained money. More money than she'd ever seen before. Fifty-dollar bills trundled into cylinders and fastened with elastic bands.

Her hands were shaking as she hurriedly counted the bundles. Fifteen in total. If each roll contained one thousand that meant the bag held fifteen thousand dollars. Amy sank forward onto her knees still holding the pouch. Her friend Maddie had said Frank and Greta were loaded, but Amy hadn't expected them to be rich enough to have that much cash in the house. But then again, what did she know? Maybe fifteen thousand was small change to the Foxhalls.

Now she really had been gone a long time. With trembling fingers she pulled the drawstring closed and replaced the pouch. Before leaving the bedroom she zipped up the canvas bag and pushed it back under the bed.

"Are you all right, Amy?" Frank asked when she reappeared in the kitchen doorway.

Her cheeks were burning. Guilt was most likely coming off her in waves. "Yes." Amy managed a smile. "Just took the stairs too fast."

"Right." Frank drew the word out narrowing his eyes. "Well, sit down and get ready to enjoy my famous chicken salad."

"Frank always hated salad." Greta was seated at the table looking Amy's way, but seeming to be staring past her.

Amy frowned, confused by Greta's comment. Before Amy could speak, Frank positioned himself between them.

"Yes, but it's good for me and keeps the waistline trim." His voice was gentle, but with his back to her Amy couldn't see his face.

"Yes," Greta responded, speaking slowly at first. "That's right. That's what I meant." The last few words came out rapidly.

As Amy watched, Frank moved around his wife, bending over her so he could kiss her cheek. It was a kiss that lingered while Greta's hand reached up to cup her husband's shoulder. There was tenderness and most obviously love in the embrace, but also something else. Amy thought it might be desperation. She wanted that sort of love so badly her chest ached.

She meant to look away and give the couple a private moment, but instead she found herself staring at Frank's head as it bent over his wife. There was a prickle of re-growth on his scalp. Until that moment she'd thought Frank was completely bald. But with the afternoon light coming through the dining room window she could see he had a full head of hair. Why, she wondered, would Frank shave his head when most men half his age would kill for that much hair? The thought was fleeting, a weird observation that for a few seconds distracted her from Greta's flash of utter confusion.

It was an awkward moment, almost odd. But Amy supposed even in its early stages Greta's illness gave birth to many uncomfortable instances. She thought of the book on the nightstand, the way the woman's fingers travelled over the piano keys and of her scars left over from a bushfire that burned half a century ago. Amy felt a wave of grief for the coming loss of all those facets of Greta's life.

With grief came the realisation that she viewed Greta as a friend and the surge of affection that came with the recognition took Amy by surprise. As she sat at the table with her elderly neighbours, she experienced the most adult emotion of her life to date: unselfish love.

Chapter Eleven

"How are the music lessons going?" Zane asked around a mouthful of pasta.

Amy longed for these evenings when he was at home and they were alone. Sharing a meal and discussing their day was a fantasy come to life. Not that Zane told her a lot about his job *or* that they had much time alone. Not while Spider was always hanging around.

"It's getting easier. Greta says I have natural ability." She knew her enthusiasm sounded child-like and boastful, but Amy didn't care.

She'd never been good at anything before. Never excelled at something or been complimented on her ability outside of her mother's unwavering belief that Amy was the most beautiful and talented girl on the planet. She'd learned early in her school career that her mother didn't see her the way the rest of the world did.

"That's great," he said. "One day I'll buy you a piano and then you can play just for me."

His words made her feel absurdly giddy. It didn't matter that the promise sounded vague and half-hearted and he was already more interested in his mobile phone.

"Greta and Frank invited us for dinner on Thursday. You could meet them." She was talking too much now. Soon he'd be telling her to shut up, but he was in a good mood so she pushed her luck. "I could play for you on their grand piano. The sound is–"

"Another time maybe." He was pulling apart a hunk of garlic bread, losing interest in the conversation.

"You'll never guess what I found in Greta's and Frank's bedroom."

She hadn't intended to tell him about the money, but at that moment regaining his attention was all that mattered. When he didn't respond, Amy pushed on.

"Maddie was right. They're sitting on a fortune," she continued.

"What?" He'd stopped chewing and was listening, his dark eyes more guarded than interested.

The shielded look in Zane's gaze gave her pause: a slight tingling of unease which almost stopped her from continuing. She'd seen that look before, but couldn't quite fathom what was going on behind his stare. Amy noted the way his fingers clenched around the fork and the alertness in his formerly relaxed posture, and thought of telling him about the book she'd found on Greta's nightstand or anything else *but* the money.

Yet, she didn't stop. Whatever was reflected in his eyes didn't matter as long as they were on her, paying attention to her, making her feel like she mattered to him.

"A bag filled with money." She paused, watching his face and relishing the way he appeared transfixed by her words. "There had to be at least fifteen thousand dollars in fifties."

That night they made love. It was the first time he'd touched her in over a week and then it had only been kissing that ended abruptly with him pulling away because he was too tired for more. But now she was in his arms, running her fingers through his thick silky hair and shivering as his breath beat out a rhythm on her neck.

Sleep came quickly, but in the early hours she woke with a start. The sheets, still damp with their shared sweat, clung to her body adding weight to the oppressive heat and smells that filled the darkened room.

As she stood and pulled on her nightdress, her mind jumped between the red rose on the cover of the book in Greta's room and the look in Zane's eyes when she told him about the money. Appalled, she saw herself pulling him into the bedroom demanding her reward. Needing air now, she padded through the house and opened the back door.

Standing on the deck feeling the rough wood under her bare feet, she took in deep gulps, breathing in the night. It would be light soon and then the birds would be singing. She'd never liked the dark. It seemed to wipe away the real world. Anything could happen in the dark.

Telling him about the money had been a mistake; she could see that now. Gossipy and indiscreet, but not harmful. Surely not. She had to believe Zane was a good man because if she didn't, what did that make her? How could she crave him so if she didn't trust he was decent and honest?

The things they'd done in the past would never happen again. She'd never let them happen again. It was a one off; Zane had promised.

"No harm done," she said wrapping her arms around her chest while watching the sky for the first signs of morning.

Chapter Twelve

Frank flipped the tarp off the bike. Everything was in place, but it never hurt to run a final check. His fingers travelled along the underside of the tank until they found the keys taped in place. He tapped the fuel gage then opened the petrol cap. Three quarters full. Finally, Frank inspected the tyres and the thick layer of mud covering the absence of a licence plate.

Exiting the garage, he glanced towards his neighbour's house. Amy would be at work and the boyfriend would be gone for hours. The young man was a concern, but not a problem. Wherever he went during the day, Frank knew it wasn't to the electrical shop. He knew because he'd made it his business to park on the nearest corner outside the Scrub Tub Laundrette, tossing back paracetamol and sipping warm coffee while he watched the shop on two separate mornings. Like re-checking the bike, it never hurt to know who you're dealing with. Or in Amy's case, who she associates with.

On the third morning, Frank let his shoulders stoop and shuffled into Markson Electronics where he spent twenty minutes feigning interest in flat screen TVs. After the second young shop assistant asked if he needed help,

Frank scratched the top of his head giving the guy his best confused pensioner routine before asking if he could speak to Zane.

Frank chuckled. "Zane really knows his stuff. Is he here?"

The young guy, whose name badge announced him as Connor, looked uncomfortable, glancing around as though hoping for someone to appear and rescue him from the conversation.

"He doesn't work here anymore." Connor slipped his hands in his pockets and then just as quickly pulled them out. "Not for a few weeks. But I can help you, if you're looking to buy a TV."

"Well, that's too bad." Frank shook his head. "Tell you what. I'll think about the TV and get back to you."

Zane was lying to Amy, Frank thought as he wheeled the trail bike off the edge of his driveway and around the left of the house to where a narrow bush trail began. Or Amy was lying to them. He'd only seen the boyfriend from a distance, coming and going with some other kid that looked like he was trying hard to look tough. Frank's gut told him Zane was the liar and that was what made the young man a concern. A concern could turn into a problem, but for now Frank thought it safe to push ahead with the plan.

The bush trail was hidden from the street by the house. In fact, if you didn't know it existed, there would be very little chance of anyone ever finding it and that's why it presented the perfect exit from Cobblestone Lane. He wasn't worried about being seen, only the effort of pushing the bike through the overgrown ruts while trying to tune out the ache in his lower back. An ache that was trying to take hold under his ribs as well as a few lumbar. Bent over gripping the handles, the pain heated up along with the temperature until every step made his torso contract.

Riding the bike would have been easier, but he couldn't risk the noise. He'd made modifications to the muffler so the engine wasn't too noisy, but even so silence was the best cover.

By the time Frank reached the other end of the trail, his shirt was stuck to his shoulders and his legs were trembling. He needed a break, but forced himself to finish what he'd started and pushed the bike off the track. Finally, he let his fingers touch the key and the tape holding it in place before he was satisfied that the old trail bike was out of sight. Staggering like a hunchback, he took a few steps to a fallen log.

Sitting was less painful than trying to straighten up, at least until his body loosened up a bit. Swiping his forearm across his brow, he dropped onto the log and let his arms rest on his thighs. Cursing himself for not thinking to bring a water bottle, Frank pulled a strip of paracetamol out of his pocked and dry-swallowed three tablets.

How long, he wondered, before he was gobbling the pills like lollies? How long before he'd have to accept the inevitable? A few months, if he was lucky. In his current situation, luck seemed like the wrong word, not that it mattered. After tonight, Greta would be safe and he could rest.

Straightening up and massaging the base of his spine, he caught sight of a dragonfly, its wings whirring in flight. Sunlight touched the insect's iridescent limbs creating a rainbow flicker that hung steady above the trail. Frank closed his eyes, enjoying the thrum of the creature's wings. A second later the sound vanished and blessedly the ache in his back and belly ebbed leaving him ready to tackle the walk home.

* * *

"Mm, lovely," Greta said, sipping her wine. "The perfect choice with salmon. Thank you, Amy."

Frank watched Greta raise her glass and smile. He also noticed the way Amy beamed back. Greta liked Amy. That was obvious and without any pretence. Hell, he liked the girl too. The liking made using her harder, but if everything went his way tonight, Amy would never have to know she'd been manipulated.

They were seated around the table in the dining room, a smaller space than the other rooms on the downstairs level, but with the highly polished jarrah table and matching credenza, it was one of Frank's most loved places. And the food. Pan-fried salmon, white asparagus and baby potatoes was one of his favourite meals. But with a ball of nervous tension sitting in his gut like barbed wire, the food held no appeal.

"Frank?" Greta held the wine bottle over his empty glass.

"Not for me," Frank said, placing his palm over his wine glass.

Greta's outstretched arm remained unmoving. The lively smile that had been in place only a moment ago was replaced by a look of confusion. He tensed watching her eyes, willing the foggy look he'd become so adept at spotting to finally lift. The pantomime they'd rehearsed was about to be enacted and for it to succeed he needed her firing on all cylinders.

"Is it…" Greta's mouth remained open, but her words stopped there.

Frank wouldn't let himself glance at Amy although he could feel her worried gaze on him. *Not tonight, sweetheart. Not now.* He kept his hand on the glass counting off the seconds. Two more seconds and he'd have to take the bottle out of Greta's hand. Two more seconds and the plan would be ruined.

"Is it your back?" Greta asked, the baffled expression lifting as suddenly as it had arrived.

Frank forced himself to wait a beat before delivering his practiced line. "Yes." He placed his knife and fork on the table beside his mostly untouched food and pushed back from the table. "I overdid the gardening today so if you ladies don't mind, I think I'll take myself upstairs and lie down."

"I'll go if you're not feeling well." Amy was already on her feet, the chair shifting so swiftly it nearly toppled.

"No, don't be silly," Frank answered with measured calmness. "It's just muscle aches and Greta's been looking forward to tonight."

He glanced at Greta hoping she'd join him in convincing their neighbour to stay, but she was looking down so he couldn't tell if the fogginess was back or if she was struggling with the pretence. Determined to push ahead, Frank took hold of Amy's chair and gestured for her to sit. The girl looked uncertain, but returned to her seat.

Upstairs, he shed his clothes and hurriedly dressed in dark pants, pulling the belt in another notch. That was two now and he supposed there'd be more to come towards the end. Weight loss would be swift or so his research on pancreatic cancer told him. Frank put on a navy bomber jacket and black boots. With a pair of dark leather gloves stuffed in his pants pocket, he was almost ready. With time to spare, he tossed down a few more pain killers then pulled the bag out from under the bed and let it sit between his feet.

Perched on the edge of the bed, he ran his hand over his scalp, feeling the bristly re-growth. He should have shaved his head. It wouldn't be wise to leave even the tiniest hair behind, but the thought was fleeting. His focus was on listening for the music. Listening and praying that Greta wasn't having one of her bad nights. Not tonight. Not when so much depended on her playing her part.

Finally, the first chords rang out and despite the tension running through him like a fever, Frank recognised Greta's touch. Lighter than when Amy attempted the piece; Greta played with a sureness that was unmistakable.

As the music scaled, he reached into his jacket pocket and found what he was looking for. Not giving himself time to hesitate, he grabbed the bag and headed downstairs.

Every floorboard and corner of the house was as familiar as the lines of his own body and with the music covering his movement, he had no trouble reaching the kitchen. Slipping out of the house, he stooped and grabbed the torch and black motorcycle helmet he'd left beside the back door.

Ten minutes to walk the trail and then an eighteen-minute drive. Twenty-eight minutes in all. Scale that up to thirty just to be on the safe side and he was looking at a one-hour round trip. That gave him another hour to take care of business and still be back by 9:40 p.m. Doable, but not much room for mistakes.

He'd left the side gate on the far edge of the garage propped open with a hunk of brick so when he exited the property he did so silently without the clink of the latch. Finding the entrance to the trail by the half-moonlight took some slow stepping, but once on the trail and inside the cover of thick shrubs and trees he turned on the torch.

The bush looked silver-grey under the artificial light and with no wind to stir the foliage the scene was oddly still. He wasn't a man to spook easily, but considering his mission the lonely sound of his boots crunching on the trail put him in mind of scattered bones. Of the long dead. At sixty-nine, Frank's memories of the long dead were now more vivid than most of the living.

A few minutes later, his light found the trail bike. Now almost a kilometre from home, he rolled the vehicle out onto the road only stopping to massage a jolt of pain out of his shoulder. He was punishing his body. Pushing the bike through the bush the day before had taken its toll. After tonight, he reminded himself as he slipped on the gloves and mounted the bike, there'd be plenty of time to take it easy. Before pulling on the black helmet and starting the engine, he flung the carry-all strap over his shoulder and let it hang at his side.

For the first few minutes he drove along mostly deserted roads, many with no street lights. It was only when the semi-rural area gave way to the outskirts of suburbia that his headlight picked up other vehicles. He was now in a part of Bunbury that holiday makers rarely saw. Shabby units and old fibrocement houses far from the ocean with its coffee shops and tourist spots. This was the Bunbury mostly inhabited by the generationally unemployed; the struggling or those that had forfeited the struggle and resigned themselves to a life of drink, drugs or desperation. For some, all three.

This was Frank's fourth visit over the last four years and each time he'd taken care to park at least a half-block away and well out of the arc of the nearest street light. Leaving the bike on these streets was a risk, but a necessary one because even in a neighbourhood where neglect was a way of life he couldn't risk someone seeing or hearing him as he approached the house. Especially not tonight.

Cutting the engine, he sat in darkness watching from a distance as a lone light shone out of a nearby house. Ron Foxhall's place sat in thigh-high weeds. Not so much a house as a tumble of bricks attached to a sagging garage. A dump with peeling paint and cracked windows topped with roof tiles faded to the colour of shower-screen mould. The thought of setting foot in the dilapidated ruin made Frank's gut contract with a mixture of dread and disgust. Dismounting the bike, he reminded himself that this would be his final visit.

Chapter Thirteen

Ron held the door open while behind him the TV blared what sounded like the hum of motor racing.

"Come in," Ron said, stepping back.

Before entering, Frank glanced at the neighbouring houses. Three things swam through his thoughts with the grim constancy of a circling shark. *Let Greta's mind stay clear. Don't be seen. God give me the strength to see this through.* The last one kept pulling ahead of the others, although he doubted God would play a part in what he was about to do.

"Did you bring it?" Ron spoke over his shoulder as Frank followed him into the house. "You'd better have it." Ron twisted his neck at an awkward angle, rheumy eyes travelling from Frank's face to the bag on his shoulder.

The house stank of cigarettes and rotting food. Frank nodded, not trusting himself to speak. Seemingly satisfied, Ron dropped his wiry frame into a cracked vinyl armchair that looked sticky with nicotine. He used the remote to mute the television.

"All right." Ron stuck a cigarette in his mouth and lit it. "Let's see."

Frank crossed the cramped room, pulling the bag off his shoulder. He unzipped the carry-all, pulled out the pouch and tossed it in Ron's lap.

"Hey!" Ron flinched as the bag knocked the cigarette out of his fingers. "Watch it, big man," he said, fumbling to pick up his still smouldering smoke and brush ash off his stained pants. "You've got a shitty attitude for someone who should be grateful."

Frank clamped his teeth together, resisting the urge to knock the cigarette out of Ron's yellowed fingers a second time. He knew what the other man meant about him being grateful, but gratitude was the least of Frank's emotions.

"Huh," Ron said, pulling the draw string and peering into the pouch. "Looks a bit light. That woman of yours keeps a tight rein on the purse strings, I bet." He gave a wheezy laugh that revealed a set of large dentures.

"It's all there," Frank said, still staring down at Ron as the man pawed over the rolls of money.

Over the past few years, Frank had come to hate Ron Foxhall in a way that was so pure and undiluted it was almost like a drug. A poisonous elixir that kept him going despite the pain. As a young man serving in Vietnam, Frank became familiar with hate and resentment. Resentment for a government that would draw his name at random and wrench him out of his life and into the hellish nightmare of a foreign jungle. Hate for the atrocities he witnessed and the constant smell of sweat and fear that clung to his skin. Yet, his feelings for Ron Foxhall made those emotions seem pale.

"A real tight ass that one." Ron was still talking. "But not too tight to let my brother knock her up behind the stables. And in broad daylight too. All scarred up like that, she was lucky he'd even touch her." He made a *hee haw* noise that sent a drill of rage though Frank's brain.

"My big brother thought he'd won the lottery marrying into that rich family. And sit down, why don't you? I don't like you standing over me." Ron leaned forward and snatched the asthma puffer off the coffee table and stuck it in his mouth.

Frank made no move to sit. Instead, he watched Ron suck in a shot of Ventolin while holding a cigarette in his other hand. Frank thought of the way his boots had crunched on the trail. *The long dead.* He couldn't shake the thought.

"How did it feel?" Ron asked with a grin. "When you got home from war and she'd married Frank? The real Frank Foxhall. The local bad boy?"

Frank kept his expression neutral. He understood Greta did what she had to. Out of some screwed up need to protect her and maybe himself, Frank told her not to wait for him when he left for Vietnam. So, when Greta realised she was pregnant, she married Foxhall and moved to Queensland. These things he understood and more importantly forgave, but that didn't mean the hurt wasn't still there.

Hurt that lasted thirty-four years. Until fifteen years ago when he returned to Bunbury after half a lifetime spent moving from place to place and job to job, he saw her. A chance meeting in a supermarket parking lot of all places. Seeing Greta older but in many ways unchanged had the power to wipe away the years *and* the hurt. Or at least dull its edges.

Within two months, Frank was dead and he, Jim Cole, had taken Frank's place. Greta's parents were gone and no one in Western Australia had seen Frank or Greta for close to thirty-five years. Jim stepped into Frank's life with surprising ease, living with Greta as her husband and sharing a love they'd been denied for so long. A type of secluded happiness he thought he'd never find. He'd been Frank for so long now he barely remembered being Jim at all. But then Ronald Foxhall was released from prison and turned up on their doorstep.

"Your big brother was a mean tempered bastard who was quick with his hands, but not with his wits." Frank bit off his words. "He got what he deserved."

"Is that right?" Ron asked, turning his face up to eyeball Frank while baring his dentures. "You think he deserved to be cuckold and murdered by that fancy talking bitch? She's a black widow that one. I hope you sleep with one eye open."

"What do you care as long as you're getting paid?" Frank knew it was pointless arguing with Ron, but the sound of his voice and the venom of his words pulled Frank into the back and forth.

Ron shrugged his narrow shoulders. "You want to keep pretending you're Frank Foxhall? You want to keep playing house with that murdering bitch? It's going to cost you. I'm just keeping it in the family." Ron pulled the draw string, closing the bag. "I'm all about family, me."

Unable to stomach Ron's face another second, Frank looked around the hovel of a room. Over the last four years they'd paid Ron over a hundred grand and by the looks of his house none of it had been spent on repairs.

"So, what have you been spending all this family money on, Ron?" Frank asked. "Not this shit tip," he added, edging his way around Ron's chair.

Time was short and Frank had wasted enough of it on a dead-end conversation. He had to act now and worry about the rest of the money later. He'd imagined what was to come next a hundred times or more. Five minutes ago, he'd been itching to hurt the man that had caused him and Greta so much anguish. A man that was draining the funds that were to be used for Greta's care once her decline really took hold. Yet, now that the moment had arrived, his heart was galloping and his mouth was dry.

"Wouldn't you like to know?" Ron's attention was still on the drawstring of the bag that nestled on his lap.

Moving around to the back of Ron's chair, Frank reached into his pocket and pulled out the thick plastic bag. The motorcycle gloves he still wore made his hands feel hot and clammy.

"What the fu–" Ron's shiny bald head swivelled in Frank's direction.

In the second before he attempted to wrench the bag over Ron's head, Frank caught a look of panic in the man's eyes. The disbelieving horror was enough to make Frank hesitate.

Ron sprang to his feet with an agility Frank hadn't seen coming. It was only his own quick reflexes that allowed him to grab the smaller man's shoulder and yank him down into the chair. Batting Ron's arms away, he dragged the plastic bag over Ron's head and drew it tight at the base of the man's skull.

He could smell fear as Ron struggled: sour and musky. A stench mixing with his own scent to create a sickening mix. Ron's hands groped at the plastic, first clawing at the bag then reaching above his head in a futile attempt to dislodge Frank's grip. The springs on the old armchair groaned as Ron bucked and twisted, but Frank held firm. Over his own rapid breath, he could hear the plastic crinkle and seal over Ron's gaping mouth.

With Frank's shoulder muscles bunched and burning with the effort of keeping the bag in place, the seconds ticked by. And with each beat Frank willed the ordeal to end. He willed the smaller man to give up his frantic fight. In the last throws of his struggle, Ron's right arm shot up and he snatched hold of Frank's sleeve, first yanking the fabric and then slapping Frank's forearm before losing strength and dropping into his lap.

Now all that remained was Frank's breathing fast and shallow as he clung to the bag. He wasn't sure how long he held tight, only that when he finally released the pressure his fingers were stiff and aching.

Sealed by saliva, the bag caught on Ron's mouth. When Frank pulled, the seal broke with a wet pop then slid off the dead man's head. The sound more than the struggle cemented what had taken place. Saliva flooded Frank's mouth as the contents of his stomach roiled.

He stumbled away from Ron, not wanting to see the man's dead face, but unable to stop himself from staring. In the stillness of the aftermath, the repulsive nature of the crime was laid bare. Ron's eyes were wide and threaded with ruptured capillaries as they stared skyward, while a string of drool hung from his lower lip.

Frank swung the carry-all off his shoulder and let it drop. Following the bag, he sunk to the floor and pressed his gloved hands into his eyes. There was no satisfaction in the act he'd committed. He'd taken lives as a soldier. In war, he'd killed in fear as well as panic and desperation because as a young man his drive for survival had been hot and imperative. This, what he'd just done, was personal: almost intimate.

Ron Foxhall was a lousy excuse for a man, but what did taking the man's life make Frank?

"Come on," Frank whispered. "Come on." He had to move. There was more to be done and so little time.

Pushing himself to keep going, he found his feet. Still breathing heavy, he swallowed the dank air already permeated by death. He forced his mind to turn to the search. Ron was a hoarder. He wouldn't risk going to a bank. He would have stashed the money somewhere in the house. Money that if found would raise alarm bells.

This wouldn't be over until he found the money and the old photographs. Swallowing the bile that sprung up in the back of his throat, Frank started the search.

Chapter Fourteen

The afternoon passed with excruciating slowness as did all shifts at the Day Mart. Of all those soul-destroying hours spent in the cut-price department store, somehow Saturdays were the worst. A sea of shoppers moved like zombies; the constant clanging of trolleys punctuated by the piercing squeals of unruly children.

Lifting boxes of kitchen appliances into a steel cage, Amy's thoughts went to Zane. The other night when she returned from the Foxhalls' house, he was already in bed. Crawling in next to him, she had the sense he was faking sleep. Since then, he'd barely been home and she'd spent the past few days trying to figure out what she'd done wrong and how she could put it right.

"Amy?" Mr Hodges had a habit of appearing behind her. "When you've finished with your cage, I want you in bedding. The shelves are a mess and we're two people short today."

"Um, I'm supposed to finish in half an hour," she said, glancing at her watch.

Hodges went silent and even without looking at him she knew he was waiting for her to make eye contact. Eye contact seemed to be his thing, which was surprising for someone who liked to sneak up behind people.

Turning away from her cage, Amy forced herself to meet his gaze. There was no tissue paper on his neck today, but she did notice a spot of dried blood on his chin and it briefly occurred to her that he should switch to an electric razor.

"If you stop clock watching, you'll find half an hour is ample time to unload those boxes and tidy up a few shelves."

"Okay." She tried to focus on Hodges, but couldn't help notice that some of the guys on the loading dock were listening as the boss delivered the reprimand.

"You need to pick up the pace or I'll have to give your shifts to someone who will," he continued in a voice she'd once mistaken for kindness but now knew was pure condescension. "There are plenty of people who are happy to work long and hard without making excuses."

Amy dipped her head, unable to bare the sight of his watery eyes a minute longer. "Sorry."

She could feel heat creeping up her neck. It was bad enough to be scolded like a child, but the fact that so many people were witnessing the moment made her want to sink into the concrete floor.

"Sorry," she said, repeating the apology, not knowing what else to say and desperately wanting the interaction to end.

"All right." Hodges sounded satisfied and confident. "Well, get to it."

It took closer to an hour to finish stacking the shelves and then work her way through the clean-up in bedding. By the time she grabbed her bag from her locker, her shoulders were aching, and the beginnings of a headache was building in the back of her skull.

It was only when she see-sawed her way down the isle of the bus to a vacant seat that she felt her bunched muscles relax. It didn't matter that the bus was jam-packed with high school kids and she was forced to sit crowded up against a window. The air was stuffy and carried a combination of so many smells it was hard to identify the most pungent. None of that mattered. The unpleasant odours were the scent of freedom and the cramped bus a chariot of escape. She leaned her head against the cold window and tried to forget Mr Hodges and the pitting stares of the men on the loading dock.

The bus stopped with a gassy jerk that made the window shudder under Amy's cheek, rousing her from an uneasy doze. A few minutes later she was walking towards the corner, heading for Cobblestone Lane while trying to fathom Zane's growing indifference and his increasing absences. Until now, she had tried to tell herself that he was feeling neglected or even jealous of her friendship with the Foxhalls or overwhelmed at his new job. The excuses for his treatment of her, even as she formulated them, were flimsy and desperate attempts to reconcile his treatment of her with something close to love.

She'd seen real love, passionate and unwavering. Affection passed between Frank and Greta that was so apparent it was like a tangible ribbon connecting them. What she had with Zane was a poor comparison. Turning the corner, she wondered how long she could continue to fool herself into believing her life was anything more than a hollow lie. A demeaning job and an absent partner – if she could call Zane her partner, because he certainly wasn't her lover.

She clutched her bag to her chest as her cheap black jogging shoes scuffed over the pavement. She needed to put her relationship woes aside and focus her thoughts on how they were going to pay next month's rent. Income from her shifts at Day Mart barely covered groceries and so far she hadn't seen a cent from Zane's new job. Another problem to be tackled when he had five minutes to spare, she thought with more than a touch of bitterness.

When the house came in view, she spotted a dark sedan parked alongside the curb and her steps faltered. It was the same car she'd seen in the Foxhalls' driveway that morning after she'd received a hurried call from Frank letting her know he wouldn't be able to make it for their usual carpool.

Something about the non-descript vehicle made her want to turn and run. Before she had time to change direction, the driver's and passenger doors swung open in unison and two men emerged. Amy's breath caught in her throat. There was no mistaking they were police. They were her nightmares come to life.

The urge to run was outweighed by the heaviness of her limbs. Not that it mattered because the two men, both wearing dark glasses, were watching her. Every second she remained unmoving made her look guiltier. *I am guilty and they see it.*

"Amy Holt?" the younger of the two asked. "I'm Detective Worsten and this is Detective Cowl. We'd like to talk to you if you have a few minutes."

She was only metres away now, close enough to see the identification both men proffered. Close enough for them to hear her rapid breathing.

"Yes." Amy was at the foot of her driveway. "Sorry, I mean of course. Come in."

The detectives perched on the edge of the sofa. Seemingly relaxed, they reminded her of lions: focused and ready to pounce. Amy sat in the armchair trying to keep still. They were in the lounge room where she was painfully aware of the stuffy air and the empty beer cans and chip packets that littered the coffee table. A leftover mess from Zane and Spider's late-night drinking session.

Part of her wanted to clear away the clutter. Bustling around the room swiping at crumbs and gathering up rubbish would be preferable to sitting under the cops' watchful gazes. Another deeper part of her was almost relieved it was finally over. So, she remained in place, hugging her elbows and pressing her shoes into the rug.

"Can you tell me where you were on Thursday night?" Worsten asked, pulling a notebook out of his jacket pocket. When he moved, Amy caught a glimpse of the gun strapped to his side and the patch of sweat gluing his shirt to his skin.

"What?" It wasn't the question she'd been expecting. "I don't understand."

Worsten gave a tight smile. "It's nothing to be concerned about. Detective Cowl and I are working on a case and just following up on some routine enquiries." He waited a beat, maybe expecting a response. "So, Thursday night?"

She was trying to follow what he was saying, but at the same time her mind was working on his question and what it might mean. She tried to remember where Zane was on Thursday. Was he at home when she left to go next door?

Worsten was waiting for an answer, his pen poised over the notebook. If she stalled any longer, he'd probably be suspicious. But wasn't suspicion the reason the cops were sitting in her lounge room? Suspicion was their business.

"I was just next door having dinner with my neighbours, Greta and Frank. Why?" She hadn't meant to ask the question, but once it was out, she was eager for an answer.

"Okay." Worsten nodded. "What time did you go next door?"

It wasn't an answer, but she didn't dare ask again.

"About seven," Amy responded, glancing at Detective Cowl. His silence was almost as unnerving as his partner's questions.

"And how long were you with the Foxhalls?"

Amy turned back to Worsten, surprised that he knew Frank and Greta's surname. She thought of the cop's dark sedan parked in her neighbour's driveway that morning and realised the detectives had already spoken to the

Foxhalls. What she didn't understand was why. What were they hoping to discover?

"I… um…" She hesitated, unsure how much to reveal. Where was Zane? If he was in trouble, why hadn't he said something? How could she help him if she didn't know what was going on? "I stayed about three hours, I think," she finally answered.

Worsten made a note in his book. "And were Frank and Greta Foxhall there the whole time?"

Amy snatched another glance at Cowl. He was older than Worsten with heavy jowls and guarded eyes that made it difficult for her to read his expression. Yet, somehow she had a sense he was listening more closely now.

"Yes, they were there the whole evening." She was about to say more when it dawned on her that the cops might not be interested in Zane at all. Was it possible they were here to question her about the Foxhalls?

"Wait." Amy sat forward. "Why are you asking me about Greta and Frank? Has something happened to them?"

The memory of the detective's car sitting on her neighbour's driveway jumped into her mind for the third time since she'd returned home to find the police waiting for her. Only now the cops' presence at the Foxhalls' house seemed more ominous.

This time it was Cowl who answered. "Frank Foxhall's brother was murdered on Thursday night. And as Detective Worsten said, we're just following routine lines of enquiry."

"Oh God." Amy forgot about trying to remain composed or how she might look in front of the cops. "Poor Frank. Murdered? That's horrible."

Her mind was racing, jumping from the shocking news to what the detectives were really doing in her house.

"Is that why you're here?" Amy asked, surprised by her own boldness. "You think Frank had something to do with his brother's murder?" She looked from Worsten to Cowl searching their blank expressions. "That's crazy. Frank was at home on Thursday. And" – she spread her hands wide – "he's a sweet, kind man. There's no way he'd hurt anyone."

"Yes." Worsten nodded. "We're simply following procedure. Eliminating people where possible so that we can focus our efforts where needed." He tapped the pen on his book. "Whatever you can tell us will allow us to do exactly that. I know this is upsetting, but I only have a few more questions. Okay?"

His voice was mechanical with no trace of emotion. He didn't give a damn about how upset she might be and for her part Amy wanted the interview to be over. She needed to talk to Frank and Greta and make sure they were okay. But mostly, she wanted the two cops out of her house.

"Okay," she said, knowing the only way to hurry things along was to co-operate.

"Now," Worsten said, glancing at his notes. "You said Frank and Greta were with you from around seven o'clock to about ten. Is that correct?"

Amy nodded her agreement. "That's right."

"Were you with both Frank and Greta the whole time?" Worsten asked.

She hesitated. "Frank's back was bothering him, so he went upstairs for a while. You know, to rest." Worsten started to write in his notebook, so she quickly added, "he didn't leave the house, though."

Worsten's pen stopped moving. "How long was he upstairs?"

Amy knew what the detective was thinking, but it was too late to change her story. Besides, Frank had probably already told them about needing to rest his back. If she said anything to the contrary, it would be an obvious lie. Not that she thought there was any reason to change her story. Still, there was something in the way the cops kept their faces expressionless that worried her.

"An hour and a half, maybe two," Amy said.

"Could he have left the house without you knowing?" Cowl asked.

She made herself wait a second before answering. "No. Definitely not. I was downstairs the whole time so I would have heard him. He often gives me a lift to work and his car runs a bit rough. There's no way he could have started it without me hearing."

"Right." It was Worsten who responded. "Did you see Frank before you left at... um..." he glanced at his notes "... at ten o'clock?"

"Yes, I did. Frank came downstairs to say goodnight just as I was leaving. He looked sleepy." She looked from Worsten to Cowl. "You know, like he'd just woken up."

Neither man responded to the last part, but when Worsten flipped his notebook closed and slipped it in his pocket, it was clear the interview was over.

Before leaving, Detective Worsten stopped at the front door and pulled a card out of his jacket. "If you remember anything else, you can contact me on this number."

A few minutes later, Amy used her finger to hold back the curtain as she watched Worsten and Cowl climb into their car and drive away. Had she done the right thing by being so honest with the cops? For Frank's and Greta's sake she hoped so.

Chapter Fifteen

"It's nothing to worry about," Frank said, sounding surprisingly like Detective Worsten. "Routine stuff. I'm just sorry they bothered you."

Greta was upstairs resting and they were in the kitchen where a bowl of apricots dominated the top of a marble-topped island block. The spacious room with its high ceilings and solid surfaces put her in mind of a farmhouse. Not surprising, given that Greta had told her how the Foxhalls' home once sat amidst paddocks and stables.

"It was nothing," Amy said waving a hand in front of her face. "I can't imagine what you must be going through, losing your brother like that. If there's anything I can do to help, I'm here."

"Thank you." Frank rapped his knuckles on the marble. "Come out back and have a beer with me."

He was smiling. When Frank Foxhall smiled, the word 'dazzling' always popped into Amy's mind. Today, exhausted seemed to better fit the bill.

"I'd love to," Amy said and waited as he grabbed two stubbies out of the fridge.

The deck was partly shaded by the gnarled branches of an apricot tree. The two of them sat at a weathered pine table and watched the sun blaze into orange as it sank in the west. Amy took a sip of beer and stretched her legs under the table. In this peaceful and secluded spot, the world seemed less complicated. When she closed her eyes against the sun and felt the heat on her eyelids, thoughts of Zane and their money woes felt like they belonged to someone else – at least for a few minutes.

"I don't know how many times we've watched the sky from this spot," Frank said, sipping his beer. "This is hard on Greta. She used to be unshakable, but these days things upset her." When he continued, there was a catch in his voice. "I'm losing her and I'm worried that all this is speeding up the process."

There were pouches under his eyes, puffy and dark. Amy thought he looked like a man trying to put on a brave face while his heart was breaking. She spent so much time worrying because her boyfriend didn't give her enough attention while Frank was coping with his ailing wife and now the murder of his brother. By comparison, her problems for the most part seemed small and petty.

"And what about you?" she asked, setting her beer down on the table. "You've just lost your brother."

"Huh." He let out a rueful laugh. "We weren't close. Ron spent most of his adult life in prison. All I care about is Greta. If anything happens to me, I need to know she has someone to turn to."

His words were unsettling. She wondered what he meant by something happening to him. He didn't look well, but Amy had put that down to the shock of losing his brother. Was there more going on than he was telling her? Did those dark pouches mean something else? The Foxhalls gave her friendship and a type of acceptance she'd never known before. The idea of losing either of them was too painful to contemplate.

"I'm here for Greta and for you. Whatever you need," she said, watching Frank's profile in the disappearing light.

"There is something," he said. "We own number two and four. As you know, four is vacant." He hooked his finger in the neck of his beer and gestured towards the street. "I don't want to have to worry about managing the rentals. Not when Greta needs me. Would you consider taking over that role? And maybe some errands like grocery shopping and that sort of thing?" He set his beer down on the table. "We'd pay you for your time. How does three hundred a week sound?"

Amy sat surprised by the question. She was willing to do whatever she could to help, but the idea of working for the Foxhalls wasn't something she'd ever considered.

"I couldn't take your money, Frank. You and Greta have been so good to me. I just want to help."

"You'd be doing us a favour." He shrugged his large shoulders. "I can see I've put you on the spot, so don't answer now. Take your time and think it over."

"All right," she said, overwhelmed by the generosity of the offer.

"You're a good person, Amy." He was looking towards the sky as he spoke. "You've already helped more than you'll ever know."

* * *

It was almost ten o'clock when Zane arrived home. When he stomped through the lounge room without a word of greeting, Amy noticed he was wearing a white T-shirt and jeans. The tight-fitting clothes accentuated his muscular frame, but also reminded her of the way Spider Crease dressed.

She thought of telling him about the cops, but why bother? They didn't ask about Zane and whatever she said would only lead to an argument.

"Amy?" he called from the other room. "What's to eat?"

She ignored the question and went to the bathroom to take a shower. She was showering more lately and couldn't help wondering if that meant anything. Fifteen minutes later she found him sitting at the kitchen table stuffing handfuls of cornflakes into his mouth.

"There's nothing to eat," he said, dumping the empty cereal box on the table.

"The rent's due next week," Amy said disregarding his complaint. "I don't have the money to pay for food *and* rent."

They'd been in Bunbury for almost a month and this was the closest she'd come to asking him to chip in on expenses. There was silence, the sort that usually came before a storm. Heat, built up throughout the day, clung to her skin like a sodden coat. As she snatched up the empty box and took it to the bin, she could feel his eyes on her. Her hands were shaking, but she wouldn't back down this time.

"You want money?" His voice was flat and angry. "Here."

He pulled a handful of notes out of his pocket and dumped them on the table. She didn't need to count the money to know there was nowhere near enough.

In that moment of watching him play the wounded party as he prepared to deliver a petulant barrage, she wondered what she was doing, not just in Bunbury, but with Zane. And what was *he* getting out of this sham of a relationship? Did he keep her close because she knew too much?

"Where do you go?" Amy asked trying to keep the tremor out of her voice. "You're never home and when you are here, *he's* always with you. What's he even doing here?" She didn't need to say his name. They both knew she was talking about Spider.

There was surprise in Zane's dark eyes. Her role was supposed to be the pathetic girlfriend: the idiot who cooked and paid the bills, someone to clean up his mess and not ask questions.

"When did Edward Crease move to Bunbury?" The questions she'd bottled up tumbled out. "When did he become part of our lives?"

"What do you want from me!" Zane screamed the words and pounded his fist on the table, making the wad of cash jump as Amy's heart raced.

She should have backed down. This was her cue to cry and beg his forgiveness. If she apologised now, there was a chance Zane would calm down; a small chance he'd pull her into his arms and tell her everything would be okay. But the memory of the men on the loading dock watching as she apologised like a scolded child still burned in her mind.

She looked him in the eye before answering. "I want my car back."

There was a moment of satisfaction, watching his face morph from anger to amazement. But the feeling was short lived. Zane jumped up with such speed that his chair toppled over.

"Fuck you," he spat then used both hands to flip the table over.

Amy jumped back, but not before the corner of the table struck her thigh. Ignoring her yelp of pain, Zane stormed out of the room. A few seconds later, the bedroom door slammed.

It wasn't the worst blow up they'd had, but it was certainly the first time she'd stood up to him. Alone in the kitchen, she bent to scoop up the money from where it had landed, except a wave of misery took her by surprise and she sank to her knees, tears blurring her vision.

What had she achieved by provoking him? A second of gratification and most likely a week of being ignored. *He already ignores me.* Yes, but now there'd be a dark cloud over the house, a sense of danger in the air until she broke down and sobbed. How long before she begged him for a kind word or gesture? A day? Less?

Take my car. I want you to use it. She could almost hear herself sweet-talking him. *Don't worry about money. I'll ask for extra shifts.*

She'd stood up to him. Didn't that mean she had somehow gotten stronger? Strong enough to use the money he'd tossed on the table to fill the car tank up with fuel and drive away? That type of courage was beyond her. She was bound to Zane by what they'd done and the destructive force that passed for a relationship.

She slumped off her knees and onto her butt. It wasn't difficult to pinpoint the moment when dating Zane had turned into something dark – something desperate and utterly unhealthy.

Chapter Sixteen

She remembered it started with her phone buzzing at 3:04 a.m. that morning. Only nine months ago and as fresh in her mind as an unhealed wound. Foggy from sleep, she'd mistaken its sound for her alarm.

"Amy?" There was fear in Zane's voice, something she'd never heard before. "Something's happened. Can you come to my place?"

He was breathing hard. Even half-asleep, she heard the panic in his voice and it acted on her like cold shock, pulling her into a hyper-alert state.

Her heart stuttered. "What is it? Are you okay?"

She remembered jumping out of bed, the phone clamped to her ear. They'd only been together for three months but already everything else, family, friends and work were falling away until Zane *was* her life.

"I need help," he said. Those three words were enough.

She arrived at Zane's house twenty minutes later to find a young man unconscious on the lounge room floor. Shirtless and with a needle sticking out of his arm, the unmoving man's jeans were open and pulled low on his hips.

Visualising that night, Zane's pale clammy face and the unconscious man's exposed body, Amy could barely remember what was said. For the first few minutes she'd simply stared at the body as though she was watching from outside of herself.

"Now!" Zane's voice snapped her out of her trance. "We need to get him in your car."

"His face is cut," Amy said, pointing to the crescent-shaped wound under his eye. "What happened to him?"

"Jesus, I don't know," Zane barked. "He probably hit it when he flaked out."

"I'm calling an ambulance," she said, pulling her phone out of her pocket.

"No!" Zane grabbed her arm. "We'll put him in your car and drive him to the hospital. It'll be quicker."

For a second, she thought she'd misheard him. It made no sense to risk taking the man in her car.

"But what if he dies?" she stammered. "He could stop breathing or have a seizure."

She couldn't tear her eyes away from the almost naked man – a body Zane wanted her to touch.

"What was he doing here?" she asked. "Who is he? Why… Why is–"

"Jesus, Amy. He's a mate." Zane ran his fingers through his hair, then pulled at his scalp. "I let him crash here. I didn't know he was going to shoot up."

"I don't think he's breathing," she continued. "We should get help. We can't just put him in the car. We can't." Her voice was getting louder, building into a scream. "He's not moving."

"Amy." Zane clamped his hands on either side of her face. "I'm on parole. If the cops see this, I'll go back inside. Is that what you want?"

She tried to wrench her face out of his grip, but he held tight, his fingers digging into her cheeks. *Parole?* Why didn't she know Zane had been in trouble with the police?

"We'll take him to the hospital," Zane said staring into her eyes. "We won't give our names. That way none of this will come back on me."

He released the pressure on her face but didn't let go. "Come on, kiddo. You've got to help me. It's the only way." He pushed a strand of hair off her forehead. When he continued, his voice was calm. "I love you, Amy. Do this for me."

She was lonely, needy even, but not completely stupid. Zane knew how she craved those words. He was manipulating her, but that didn't mean he loved her any less, did it?

She closed her eyes and nodded. "Okay."

His lips, feverishly hot, pressed against her mouth. Despite what was happening she felt a shiver of pleasure and then immediate shame.

Before they carried the body to the car, Zane dashed into the kitchen and returned with a paper towel. Amy watched in horror as he wrapped the napkin around the needle and pulled it out of the guy's arm.

"It's better that we bring it, so they know what he's taken," he said, setting the syringe down on the coffee table.

Touching the man's bare ankles made her cringe. His skin was cool and almost felt like plastic. As they shuffled out of the house and into the night's darkness, Zane's head swivelled back and forth.

"Get back," he hissed.

Amy stumbled back, pressing her shoulder into the bushes near the front of the house. A second later a car crested the slight hill, its lights scooping by only metres from where they stood. Amy's arms shook and the man's ankles slid out of her grasp.

"Pick him up." Zane's voice, a panicked whisper, came out of the dark. "Grab his feet."

She scrambled down, feeling for the guy's feet only to pull away when she felt cold skin.

"Hurry up." Zane was a dark outline. "When we get to the car, turn off the interior light."

Amy grabbed the man's ankles and they moved towards the car. Zane held the guy's upper body while she opened the back passenger door then ducked inside to do as he had instructed. A minute later, the unconscious man was on the back seat. Zane disappeared and returned moments later holding the syringe. Before starting the car, he put the needle, still wrapped in the paper towel, in the cup holder between them.

They drove in silence. Zane's head kept moving, checking the mirrors as if someone was following them. Amy slumped against the door, rubbing her fingers back and forth across her lips while her mind jumped between the young man's almost naked body on the floor of her boyfriend's house to the waxy feel of the guy's ankles in her hands. It was wrong. Everything about what they were doing was wrong.

She should have insisted they call an ambulance. Whatever Zane's reasoning, transporting the man themselves was only making matters worse.

While the streets were almost eerily deserted, when the occasional headlights came into view, she braced herself for the wail of sirens and the flash of blue lights.

Nearing the intersection of Draper Road, deep wet-sounding gurgles cut through the silence. Amy turned in her seat, peering into the back of the darkened car. The young man's pale body jerked as his choking escalated.

"He's choking, Zane. Do something."

"What do you want me to do?" Zane asked. "I'm driving."

She turned back to Zane, stunned by his inaction and at the same time hopelessly out of her depth.

"Pull over," she said, unclipping her seat belt. "He'll choke if we don't do something."

"Not here!" Zane's voice came out as shrill and barely recognisable. "There's too many cars around."

"I don't care. Pull over."

Maybe it was the desperation in her voice, or it could have been the wheezing rattles of the man's struggle to breathe that convinced Zane to do as she asked. He threw the vehicle into a sudden turn, tossing her against the passenger door as he veered off the main road and into the entrance to Weary Lakes.

She expected him to stop, but instead he sped up, headlights picking up a narrow road and dense bush as they headed deeper into the park.

"Pull over!" She was almost screaming now. "Stop. Let me help him."

Zane braked hard and the car came to a shuddering halt. Hands out, Amy managed to catch herself on the dashboard and avoid hitting the windscreen. She then flung open the back door only to realise the interior light was still out.

"Turn the light on. I can't see anything."

In the darkness, her splayed fingers found the man's legs. A second later, the light came on and flooded the car with an unnatural yellow glow. He was gagging, but softer now, the sound too similar to a kitten mewing. Milky bubbles filled his gaping mouth and vile liquid covered his chin and cheeks.

"What do I do? What do I do?" Amy spoke to herself as much as to Zane. "Zane?" She looked around, but the car was empty save for her and the choking man.

She had a vague memory of her mother talking about clearing someone's airway, but just how to achieve that was beyond her. Acting on impulse and with help from Zane not forthcoming, Amy climbed onto the back seat, determined to reach the man's face, but found little room to manoeuvre in. Bracing one leg on the floorboard and the other over the guy's torso brought her too close. The smell of vomit and sweat filled the inside of her nose and mouth. When she touched his face, the noises stopped, leaving just the sound of her racing breath. She used her fingertips to turn his face to the left, then pulled back as a stream of bile dribbled onto the seat.

That was good. The liquid leaving his mouth was a good sign. She hesitated, praying he'd cough or breathe or give any sign he was still alive.

"He's dead." Zane's voice held little emotion, but too much certainty.

"No. No, he's not dead," Amy said, not willing to take her eyes off the motionless man.

She needed to think. There had to be something they could do. Then it occurred to her that the angle was wrong. To really clear his throat and get him breathing again they had to move him onto his side.

"We have to get him on his side." She turned her head, but couldn't see Zane. "Zane?"

Not daring to waste any more time, she grabbed the man's shoulders and gave a hefty pull, but with her weight on top of him and the close confinement, all she'd managed was shaking his head from side to side.

"Stop it. I told you he's dead." Zane was behind her now, wrapping his hands around her waist and dragging her out of the car.

She remembered how it felt to struggle in Zane's arms and the way his grip was like an iron clamp holding her in place until the struggle left her exhausted. Everything that followed was recalled only in snatches. Her misty breath billowing out into the cold night air. Driving to the park's toilet block. The squat concrete building under a circle of halogen light amidst the dense silence of parkland.

There were other memories. A sudden cry from the lake as a startled water bird stirred. Carrying the body into the men's room only to find the entrance barred by a cyclone wire gate. The faint scent of the dead man on her skin, musky and male. The sound of Zane grunting as they placed the young man's body in the toilet block doorway. The most frightening remembrance came from the sudden drop in temperature as she watched Zane unwrap the syringe and put it next to the guy's arm. The sense of something cold filled her gut as they drove away in silence.

"What was his name?" Amy asked, staring at the nothingness filled by night.

Zane took his time answering. "Travis something."

They didn't speak again until he pulled up to his house.

"You need to clean the back seat," he said, not looking at her. "Don't tell anyone, not even your mother."

When she didn't answer, her grabbed her forearm and squeezed. "You're in this as much as me." His tone softened, but his grip remained tight. "All I want is to keep you safe. I can only do that if you promise not to say anything."

"Okay." She shrugged off his hand and rubbed her skin that still burned from the pressure of his fingers.

"Say it, Amy," he insisted. "Say, 'Zane, I won't say anything.'"

She wanted this endless night to be over. More than anything, she wanted to erase the memory of Travis's lifeless body from her mind.

"Zane, I won't say anything."

In the months that followed she had kept that promise.

Chapter Seventeen

She was surprised to hear the shower running. Zane hadn't been washing much lately or maybe he'd never been that clean and she just hadn't noticed. She opened the door of the spare room and slipped out, hoping he'd take his time in the bathroom, at least enough time for her to make coffee and change out of the clothes she'd slept in.

"Rough night?" Spider asked.

He was spooning sugar out of an open packet, dumping mounds into a mug. As the spoon moved back and forth, white granules skittered over the kitchen counter.

"Want coffee?" he asked, holding up his cup, his eyes travelling over her rumpled clothes. "You look like you need it."

She wasn't surprised to find him in the house, but wished she'd been smart enough to change before venturing into the kitchen.

"No." She didn't bother to hide her contempt. "What are you doing here, Edward?"

He picked up the kettle and filled his mug with hot water, the entire process being done with an air of ownership.

"I'm here," he began, blowing steam off the surface of his cup, "because our boy needs a lift."

Our boy.

He was hitting back at her because she called him Edward. Most things about Spider were a mystery, but the one thing she knew is how he hated being called by his real name. A petty shot on her part, but what else did she have? Still, knowing he was trying to hurt her didn't take the sting out of his words.

There was a smirk on his lips as he sipped his drink. She'd bought the coffee and the sugar he was guzzling, the money earned hauling heavy boxes while Hodges ordered her about like a slave. Amy had the urge to slap the cup out of Spider's hand. Would that wipe the smile off his face?

Instead, she did her best to ignore him, examining the meagre contents of the fridge. She wanted to slink out of the room and hide until Spider took *their boy* and left. But she wouldn't let herself take the coward's way out, not this time. Finding a couple of slices of stale bread in the pantry, she popped them into the toaster.

"I hear you've been making friends with the neighbours," Spider said, still leaning against the counter and sipping coffee. "Smart move."

"What are you talking about?" As much as she hated the sight of him, she forced herself to look his way.

He posed for her in his tight shirt, biceps bulging. She briefly wondered if it was exhausting always trying to make it look as if everything he did was effortless to him.

"A pair of childless geriatrics looking for someone to leave all that money to?" He raised his free hand. "Way to go, Amy."

The taunting tone in his voice set her teeth on edge. He was waiting now, his pale eyes aglow daring her to take the bait, hoping she'd get defensive or better still cry. In some ways she couldn't blame him. She *was* an easy target and he was a bully. They were the perfect combination, but not today.

Somewhere between grovelling around on the kitchen floor picking up the money Zane had tossed her way and waking up to find Spider making himself at home inside the kitchen, she'd made a decision. It was difficult to pinpoint the exact moment when she decided this would be the last day she played the game. Maybe the impetus for change came when she was sobbing into her pillow and trying to figure out how she let things get so out of control.

Spider was waiting for her to say something, but she wouldn't give him the satisfaction. It was better to ignore his attempts to goad her and let him watch as she spread margarine on her toast.

"Did you flutter those big blue eyes at old mate next door? Next thing you know" – Spider snapped his fingers as he moved closer – "Amy gets everything she ever wanted. Do you let the old boy *do* things to you?"

He was behind her now, reaching over her shoulder to snatch a slice of toast. His closeness made the skin on the back of her neck prickle.

"Quiet little Amy. Who'd have thought you had it in you to work those oldies?" His voice was softer now, almost a hiss. "But we know you're capable of doing whatever it takes, don't we?"

He was crowding her, breathing down her neck until she couldn't take it another second. He knew. Of course, he knew. The realisation Zane had told him what she'd done with Travis all those months ago didn't surprise her.

"Get out of my way." Amy spun around.

A glint appeared in his eyes. He could see his attempts to intimidate her were working. He placed one hand on either side of her, pinning her against the counter.

"Hey," Zane called from the doorway, his dark hair damp and combed off his face.

Spider, unhurried by Zane's arrival, took his time moving out of Amy's way. She hesitated, expecting Zane to say more, hoping he'd come to her defence. But nothing more was said until she rushed past Zane with Spider's voice ringing in her ears.

"What's her problem?"

She didn't wait to hear Zane's reply. She'd been stupid to think he'd stand up for her. Even now, after everything that had happened between them, she still wanted him to be there for her. When would she ever grow up and realise she meant nothing to him?

By the time she grabbed clean clothes and ducked into the bathroom, she was holding back tears. What would have happened if Zane hadn't walked into the kitchen when he had? She'd seen something in Spider's eyes that really terrified her – something cruel and vicious. She had no doubt he was capable of violence.

Maybe it was the encounter with Spider or the scene with Zane the previous night, but Amy was beginning to feel like the walls were closing in around her. She was out of her depth and maybe even in danger.

One minute under the shower and the water turned into an icy blast. *Thanks, Zane.* While shivering she dried herself and got dressed. With any luck Zane and Spider would be gone when she emerged from the bathroom and she'd have time to think through her plan.

She still loved Zane, but the constant battle for his attention was turning her into someone she barely recognised and someone she didn't like. The decision to take Frank's job offer and ask Zane to leave seemed so clear in the early hours. Now in the morning light she wondered if she'd have the gumption to follow through.

It would be easier to say nothing, to wait until Zane was out of the house then pack her things and go back to Perth. She could put the whole mess behind her without having to confront Zane. But Frank and Greta needed her. She was important to them and that was something she couldn't turn her back on. Helping them was a chance to do something good, a chance to make up for what she'd done.

You're in this as much as me. Zane's words from that endless night. He was right. She *was* as guilty as him. She could have stopped. She should have said no and insisted they take Travis to hospital.

Wiping the steam off the mirror then rubbing her hair dry, she heard a knock at the front door.

"Amy?" Zane called from the kitchen. "Get the door."

They were still in the house, still hanging around. Zane was closer to the door than her but unwilling to move and answer it. She tossed the towel on the rack and went to the door.

With her hand on the knob she thought of the two detectives who had questioned her the day before. The idea of facing them on top of everything else was exhausting.

Another knock, this time hard enough to shake the wood.

"Amy!" There was anger in Zane's voice. "Get the damn door."

It wasn't the detectives, but Greta.

"I don't know where Jim is. I… I don't know where he went." She looked around, one hand outstretched towards the street. "I have to visit my father."

Amy took in her dishevelled appearance and her stomach dropped. "Come in."

She reached for Greta's arm, but the older woman pulled away. "I don't know you. I want Jim." The last words were pleading, almost child-like.

"Who is it?" Zane came up from behind her and pulled the door wider.

Greta shrank back with wide eyes. "Who's he? I don't know these people."

"It's okay, Greta," Amy said, ignoring Zane. "Come in and we'll work it out."

Greta looked unsure, but took Amy's hand. To Zane, Amy said, "Just leave me alone with her."

A moment later, she had Greta settled on the sofa. There was an air of energy about the woman as though whatever clouded her mind also compelled her to move. Watching her wring her hands and stare around the room put Amy in mind of a beehive with its constant inward and outward movement.

Amy took hold of one of Greta's fidgeting hands. She spoke slowly, hoping to calm Greta's distress. "Tell me who you're looking for. Is it Frank?"

Greta gave a half nod then shook her head. "I have to visit my father. It's his birthday." She squeezed Amy's hand. "Will you take me?"

Amy had no idea what Greta was talking about and without Frank she had no idea what she was supposed to do.

"Okay, of course I'll take you," Amy said. "But first we need to tell Frank."

"No. No, no." Greta tried to stand. "I have to go now."

Amy recognised the frantic look in Greta's eyes. She'd seen it that first day when she'd taken the scones to their house. Rather than fear, she now felt protective towards Greta. Knowing Zane and Spider were in the next room probably listening to Greta's jumbled pleas made Amy uneasy. The best thing she could do for her neighbour was to get her out of the house.

"Okay," Amy said, still holding the woman's hand. "We'll go now."

She had other less altruistic reasons for agreeing to help. Amy wanted to put some distance between herself and Zane. Distance would give her time to think. Time to prepare for what would be one of the most difficult conversations of her life, telling the man she was still in love with that their relationship was over.

Once she was in the car with Greta, Amy had no idea where they were going.

"It's on O'Dare Road," Greta said, sounding calmer, almost like her old self.

As they pulled out of Cobblestone Lane, Amy had the feeling she was on a fool's errand, but she'd promised Frank she would take care of Greta so that's what she intended to do. Thinking of Frank, Amy made a mental note to call him the moment they reached their destination. When they left the house, she noticed his car wasn't in its usual place on the driveway. It wasn't like him to disappear, especially if Greta was having a bad day.

"Where now?" Amy asked, with little hope the trip was anything more than the consequences of Greta's misfiring neurons.

"I'm not sure." There was panic in Greta's voice. "This looks wrong. It's all wrong," she said, pressing her fists into her temples. "Where are we going?"

Amy thought about pulling over and calling Frank, but with every second that passed Greta seemed more agitated. If she stopped the car, Greta might try to run. Why had she thought it was a good idea to take someone as unwell as Greta for a drive? *Because I was looking for a reason to escape Spider.* She'd let him push her into doing something reckless and stupid.

"We're going to get ice-cream," Amy said, trying to watch the road and keep an eye on Greta at the same time. "What's your favourite flavour?"

"Take me home." Greta grabbed the steering wheel, her nails raking over Amy's forearm.

Without thinking, Amy jerked Greta off and at the same time turned the wheel. The car veered right and into the opposite lane and towards an oncoming van. Amy saw the other driver's shocked face. His mouth opened in surprise and the van's silver grill grew larger as it bore down on her. All these snatches occurred almost simultaneously.

Amy gasped or maybe she screamed. Sound made no sense over the blare of the driver's horn. She spun the wheel left and jammed on the brake. In response, the car shuddered, turning sideways in a surreal skid that somehow missed the van by centimetres.

Still travelling out of control, the car bounced over the curb and came to a jarring halt. The near miss was over in less time than it took for Amy to draw a shaky breath. Next to her, Greta was sobbing softly. Head down, the old lady's silky white hair covered her face.

"I'm sorry, Greta." Amy wasn't doing much of a job of holding back her own tears. "I'll take you home, okay?"

Greta seemed to be beyond hearing and continued to weep. Shaken up and with her heart sitting somewhere in her throat, Amy checked her mirrors before reversing the vehicle off the curb. Determined to get them both home in one piece, she edged the car into a slow U-turn and drove back to Cobblestone Lane.

Mercifully, Greta remained still during the short journey and at the same time light years removed from the charming, accomplished woman Amy had come to care for.

"We're home," Amy said opening the passenger door. "Let's get you inside and I'll make us some tea."

Greta raised her head and took in her surroundings. Her eyes were focused and clear, but she simply nodded and stepped out of the car. They were parked on Amy's drive. Spider's black Holden was on the street out front. As they approached the Foxhalls' house, she could see Frank's car was still absent and she briefly wondered if Greta had locked the front door. Amy didn't know of a spare key but hoped there'd be a window open on the ground floor.

As it turned out, Greta had left the front door not only unlocked, but open. There was an upturn in the breeze making the usually cool veranda a chilly wind tunnel as wayward leaves rushed around their feet. Realising no one was home, Amy felt a slight quiver of trepidation – trepidation that was instantly engulfed by relief that the horrendous morning wasn't going to culminate in her having to break into her neighbour's house.

As they were about to enter the house, Greta came to a standstill on the doorstep.

"Amy, I'm sorry we've dragged you into all this. I really am." Her tone was earnest with no trace of confusion. "I'm fine now. You don't have to babysit me."

In that moment, Amy thought she saw a glimpse of what Greta's illness was doing to her. Still in its relatively early stages, but not as early as Frank wanted to believe, Alzheimer's was a monster with its sharp talons firmly embedded in Greta's brain. As Amy watched the old lady struggle to regain her wits, she said, "I haven't been dragged into anything. We're friends and that's all there is to it." Amy gave Greta's shoulder a gentle rub, noticing how frail the woman's frame felt beneath her silky blouse. "I don't know about you, but I could do with a cup of tea."

Greta gave a weary smile. "I had a daughter once. She only lived for three weeks, but I would have been proud if she'd grown up to be like you."

Greta's words, so heartfelt, pierced Amy's heart making her feel absurdly flattered and ashamed at the same time: ashamed of the things she'd done, terrible things that turned her inside out with guilt.

Her neighbour believed she was a Good Samaritan when in truth she was the antithesis of good. She'd let a young man die because she didn't want to lose her boyfriend. She was the worst kind of selfish. Even what she was doing now was more about her own misguided attempts at redemption than it was about helping Greta and Frank.

"I'm sorry about your daughter," Amy said. "But I'm no saint."

Her mouth was trembling and her body weak. The lack of sleep from the previous night, the ugly scene with Zane, and then the weirdly frightening confrontation with Spider seemed to hit her in some sort of delayed reaction. All of it filled her mind like black ink until all that was left was misery. That and guilt.

"None of us are without sin," Greta responded. "It's not what you've done in the past, but who you become in the future. I've learned that the hard way." She took Amy's hand. "Enough shilly-shallying on the doorstep. Let's make that tea."

Chapter Eighteen

"How long will this take?" Frank asked as he followed Worsten into an interview room. "My wife's unwell and I don't like leaving her alone."

"Just a few questions." Worsten gestured to a chair before seating himself on the other side of the table.

Frank let out a sigh and sat opposite the detective, noticing the manila folder on the table to the cop's right. He wasn't surprised when Worsten called and asked him to come to the station for some follow-up questions. As the person the world believed to be Ron's closest living relative, he knew the cops would put him under a microscope.

Before speaking, Worsten made a show of checking his watch and then pulling his phone out of his jacket and placing it face down on the table. Frank guessed this was part of the man's interrogation technique, moves designed to make the suspect aware of how serious this talk was going to be.

"When was the last time you saw your brother?" Worsten had asked the same opening question the day before when he and the other detective called at the house.

"As I told you yesterday, I haven't seen my brother in months."

Worsten pursed his lips and nodded. Under the harsh fluorescent light, his pale crew cut looked almost colourless. "Your brother's neighbour, Len, said that Ronald mentioned coming into a large amount of money. When you saw him a few months ago, did he tell you where that money came from?"

Frank shrugged. "No."

Worsten held his gaze for a few seconds before opening the folder. "Three weeks ago, Ronald paid cash – eighteen thousand dollars for a used late model Holden."

The detective pulled a sheet of paper out of the file and slid it across the table. Frank glanced down long enough to see the paper was a receipt for a used car. He hadn't bothered to check in Ron's garage, but it didn't surprise him that Ron would spend big on a car while leaving his house in disrepair.

Frank folded his arms and leaned back in the chair. "I don't have my glasses with me."

Worsten nodded, retrieved the paper, and put it back in the file. "Ronald had less than four hundred dollars in his account when he was murdered. There's no sign of large deposits or withdrawals. Do you have any idea where a man in your brother's situation would get eighteen thousand dollars?"

Again, Frank shrugged. "The only time my brother had money was just before he was arrested for armed robbery. I deliberately distanced myself from Ron a long time ago so, to answer your question, no. I have no idea what was going on in my brother's life. I don't know and I don't care."

"That's pretty cold," the detective said. "I mean he was your brother. The way his neighbour tells it, Ron had a real hero worship thing going for you. According to Len, he and Ron were drinking buddies and when Ron had a few beers under his belt he'd tell stories about you back in the day. He described you as a real tough guy."

Frank didn't like where Worsten was heading. Nor did he like the idea of Ron getting tanked up and spilling his guts to the bloke next door.

"Were you?" Worsten asked and smiled. With his pale hair and small eyes, the smile made Frank think of a white pointer.

"Was I what?" Frank managed to keep his tone calm, but it was taking some doing.

"Were you a tough guy?" Worsten spoke slowly, separating each word.

"Ron was a fantasist. He liked the sound of his own voice," Frank said, ignoring the cop's question. He used Worsten's technique and checked his watch. "If there's nothing else, I need to get home to my wife."

"Just a few more minutes," Worsten replied. "We spoke to your neighbour." He flicked through the file and then pulled out another sheet of paper. "Amy Holt confirmed that she was with you and your wife on the night your brother was murdered. Although she did say that you spent a few hours upstairs resting. Did you leave the house during those hours?"

So, Frank thought, this was the real reason Worsten had called him to come to the station. He wanted to know if Frank had slipped out of the house and murdered his brother. The question wasn't a complete surprise, but hearing it on the detective's lips made Frank's pulse jump.

There were many reasons he could cite. Reasons why it was impossible for him to have done what the cop was suggesting. But he planned to stick as closely to the truth as possible. Something that made him appear vulnerable, no matter how bitter a pill to swallow, was exactly what the situation called for.

"Look," Frank said, leaning his elbows on the table. "I'm sixty-nine years old and have stage three pancreatic cancer. I'm in no condition to shimmy down the drainpipe, if that's what you're thinking."

For the first time since the cop turned up on his doorstep, Frank thought he seemed genuinely thrown.

"I see. I'm sorry to hear that." There was sympathy in the cop's voice, maybe even regret. Frank hoped it was genuine.

"Thank you," Frank said. "As a matter of fact, I'm feeling a bit fatigued. Could we wrap this up?"

Worsten nodded and closed the folder. "Of course."

The detective insisted on walking Frank to his car. The cynical part of his mind wondered if Worsten was using the walk to gauge Frank's fitness. The idea might be a bit paranoid, but still he walked slowly.

"What you said about your brother only having money when he'd committed a crime could mean he was still in that life. Could be he pissed off the wrong people."

"Could be," Frank responded, echoing the cop's words.

They were nearly at his car and Frank resisted the urge to pick up his pace. He wanted the discussion to end so he could get in his Mazda and swallow enough paracetamol to take the edge off the pain that was blossoming in his belly.

"Pancreatic cancer." The detective sounded more human now. "That's a bitch."

A bitch? Frank had never thought of the disease that way, but it seemed like an apt description. A bitch on horseback turning your insides black and carrying you to hell. Because hell, he now feared, was his final destination.

"Yes." Frank opened the driver's door. "That it is."

"Sorry I had to drag you down here. Hopefully, we'll get a break on the case, so I won't have to trouble you again," Worsten said and stuck out his hand.

Frank obliged the man by shaking it. Either Worsten was the Meryl Streep of Bunbury or he'd been touched by the same bitch that had Frank in her clutches. He guessed it was the latter.

"Take care," the detective said before turning and heading back inside the station.

Chapter Nineteen

It was considerably cooler inside. The Foxhalls' house was *always* cooler than the rest of the world. When Amy closed the door, there was a chill in the air.

"What's that?" Greta spoke over her shoulder as she continued walking along the hallway.

Amy's first instinct was that Greta was confused again, but then she too heard a noise: a metallic click, like the sound of an old-fashioned latch being lifted.

"Greta." Amy wasn't sure why she was whispering. "Greta, wait."

Either she didn't hear Amy or was choosing to ignore her. Not hesitating, Greta picked up pace heading towards the rear of the house. Amy glanced back at the now closed front door. It was open when they arrived, an invitation anyone could have taken advantage of.

"Wait!" This time Amy raised her voice and hurried after Greta.

Greta reached the kitchen ahead of Amy and disappeared from sight.

"Who are you?" Greta's voice echoed in the hallway, loud and frantic. "What are you doing here?"

Someone was in the house!

Amy rushed forward, feet pounding the hardwood floor at the same time she dragged her phone out of her pocket. All the while her pulse whooshed in her ears like wave after wave crashing on a rocky shore.

"Stop her!" a male voice Amy instantly recognised shouted, bringing her to a skidding halt as she lurched into the kitchen.

When she reached the room, Greta was in motion. Turning and locking eyes with Amy, Greta attempted to run. Zane and Spider were also on the move.

Eyes still locked, there was a moment when Greta tried to speak. Her mouth was open. A plea for help half-formed on her lips. Then a hand. Everything after that rushed together. Greta was lunging forward in an obvious attempt to escape the two men when she fell. Her forehead hit the marble-topped island with a sickening crack. Without realising she'd moved, Amy's arms were outstretched, but not fast enough to prevent the impact or to catch her friend as Greta's head bounced off the bench top and her body dropped. A china bowl filled with apricots tumbled off the island and shattered on the floor, sending fruit thumping around Greta's unmoving form.

Amy let out a scream and dropped to her knees. The phone, all but forgotten in her hand, slid to the floor. Blood was already pooling around Greta's head.

"Greta?" Amy crawled closer. "Oh my God. Greta?!"

Arms grabbed Amy from behind and for an instant the ghastly scene was replaced with an equally horrific vision of the back of Amy's car as Travis spluttered out vomit. Amy bucked and twisted her body, desperate to break free of the hands that had grabbed a hold of her so she could reach her friend.

"Calm down."

Spider's arms tightened around her, clamping her arms to her sides and his body to hers.

Tears blurred her vision and made Zane's movements waver as she watched him step around Greta's spreading blood to retrieve Amy's phone from where she'd dropped it.

"Call an ambulance!" Amy shouted, still trying to pull out of Spider's grasp. "Zane, please! She's not moving. You have to let me–"

"Shut up and listen." Spider's mouth was close to her ear.

Amy shook her head trying block out his voice and the stench of his cigarette-smelling breath. The more she struggled, the tighter he squeezed. With his fists locked between her breasts it was difficult to catch her breath. He gave a grunt and the pressure increased until Amy heard something crack and a bolt of agony run through her chest.

"This was an accident," Spider whispered calmly. "The old bird fell. If we start calling for help, there'll be questions. It'll look like you planned all this. No one will believe you weren't involved."

With breathing now a painful struggle and the sight of Greta's blood still pooling on the floor, Amy couldn't keep up with what Spider was saying. She looked to Zane silently pleading for help, but he wouldn't look at her. His attention was on her phone as he shoved it in his pocket.

It was then she spotted the grey carry-all draped over Zane's shoulder. Suddenly, everything made sense. They were here for the money. They'd waited for an opportunity when the house was empty. Was there ever any doubt this would happen?

The minute she opened her big mouth and told Zane about the money she knew it could come to this. Despite what had just happened, it was the grey bag that made her realise that she might be in danger. Amy's stomach cramped.

"I'm going to…" She started to gag before she could finish.

Still holding her, Spider lifted her off the floor and hauled her towards the kitchen sink. It was only then that his grip loosened. She slumped over the sink as vomit rushed out of her mouth and hit the plug hole.

Without Spider's arms around her, she sank until she sat on the floor. Above her, Spider pulled up his T-shirt and used the end of it to cover his hand while he turned on the tap. At the same time Zane bent over Greta and pressed his fingers to her neck.

"She's dead," he said, then stumbled backwards. "I think she's actually dead."

Amy clamped her hands over her ears and let out a shuddering wail. It couldn't be happening. Not again. Not to Greta. She allowed herself to look at her friend. Greta's head was turned to the side, one eye visible. Mercifully, that eye was mostly closed.

"We need to get out of here now. Before old mate gets back," Spider said, not to Amy, but to Zane.

The words were no sooner out of his mouth when there was a sudden rap on the front door. Amy let out a sob and pulled her knees up to her chest.

"Shit. Keep her quiet," Spider said, pointing at Amy before heading into the hall.

Alone now, Amy looked to Zane. "Please, you can't do this. It's not you. You're not like him."

Zane stood near Greta's body, his hands laced in his hair and tugging at his scalp. He appeared uncertain and almost detached, so Amy clambered onto her feet. When he made no attempt to stop her, she rushed to Greta's side.

Taking care to avoid the blood, Amy crouched down and touched Greta's face. Greta's skin was warm, but there was no sound. One of her once mesmerising green eyes was partially visible under a dropping lid. Amy had brought Zane and Spider into her neighbour's life and now she was dead. Another victim of Amy's twisted relationship.

"Greta?" She traced her fingers over the woman's silky white hair. "I'm so sorry."

"Mailman," Spider said, striding back into the kitchen. "He left a package on the veranda, but he didn't see anything. We'll give it a minute and then get out of here."

Amy wiped her eyes with the back of her hand. "You need to put the money back or Frank will know this was no accident."

"Fuck." Zane drew the word out through clenched teeth.

If it wasn't so tragic, Amy thought it might be funny. Had the two of them really thought Frank wouldn't connect the missing money to his wife's sudden death?

"We're taking the money," Spider insisted. "I don't care what the old guy thinks. There's nothing to connect us to any of this."

"But, but..." Zane spluttered. Amy had never heard him do that. "What if–"

"Just bring the money and let's go." Spider grabbed Amy's arm and turned his attention her way. "Get up or this is going to turn into a double tragedy."

As he pulled her to her feet, she saw his eyes go to the fresh scratches on her arm. "What are these?"

"It's nothing," Amy said, no longer bothering to try and resist as he dragged her closer. "Greta was upset in the car. She didn't mean to do it."

He leaned his face closer and a smile lifted his features. "That means your skin's under her nails. You'd better hope the old man thinks this was an accident or you'll be in deep shit."

His words hit her like a punch to her gut. He was right. She would be the first person the police would look at. Amy had been in and out of the Foxhall house for over a month. Greta trusted her so she'd have thought nothing of letting Amy into the house. One look at her finances would show she needed money. Put that together with her DNA under Greta's fingernails and she'd be the prime suspect.

For the last few minutes she'd harboured some hope of playing along with Spider and Zane until she could go to Frank or the detective and explain what happened. Now, any thought of putting all this right evaporated, leaving her with no choice but to do as Spider instructed.

Zane went first, moving through the front garden. He stopped at the footpath, checking to see if the street sat clear before gesturing for them to follow. Amy, wincing at the pain in her ribs from where Spider had grabbed her, scurried after the two men. With no one in sight, they moved onto the deserted street and back to number five.

***

Shell shock. She'd heard the term used to describe someone who couldn't make their mind cope with the things they'd seen and done. Was this what it felt like? That couldn't be right because she was aware of her own feelings. Sitting on the back deck wrapped in a blanket, she couldn't stop shivering nor was she able to pull the pieces of what had happened into something that made sense.

Feeling both numb and agitated, she watched the purple Jacaranda blossoms tremble in the breeze. Zane and Spider were inside, their voices low and hurried. They were making plans – ones she prayed didn't involve her. Or maybe she should be hoping their plans did include her.

Only hours ago the way ahead had seemed clear: tell Zane it was over; ask him to leave so she could restart her life. Do something worthwhile so she might make amends for her sins. Now those plans were like dry leaves.

Among all the jumble, her mind kept coming back to Frank. It was only a matter of time, minutes even, before he walked into that house and found his wife's body. *I'm losing her*, that's what he'd said only yesterday. Remembering those words made Amy's skin prickle with gooseflesh.

"Hey." Zane touched her shoulder. "You okay?"

Amy turned and looked up to where he stood. With the late morning sun behind him, it was like she was seeing him for the first time. *Really* seeing him. He was on the short side, always wearing boots with a small heel or thick soled joggers, carefully tousled hair, desperately trying to look like some outdated idea of a tough guy: some outward image that belied the fear in his eyes.

"Yes," Amy said. "I'm okay." She stood trying not to show how much her ribs hurt from Spider's rough handling.

"That's good," he said, drawing her into his arms.

She wanted to recoil from his touch and scream at him for bringing Spider into their lives and tell him to never touch her again. Despite all she'd endured, she bit back her words and allowed him to embrace her.

"It's going to be okay if we stick together. I know Spider was tough on you, but that's just his way."

Breaking my rib is just his way, she thought. "I know," Amy found herself saying.

"The worst is over," he continued, rubbing the small of her back. "We just have to get through the next few days and it will be full moons and red balloons."

Those words made her shrivel inside as he led her into the house where Spider lounged with his feet propped on the kitchen table. There was no doubt who was the boss. The house. Zane and Amy. They were all now dancing to Spider's tune.

"There's nearly a hundred grand there." Spider pointed to the pile of cash on the table. "No one keeps that kind of money under their bed unless they're hiding something. No way the old guy's going to report this money missing."

The bag sat on the table. Rolls of money were stacked next to a handful of old photographs. This, Amy thought, is what a life is worth. She'd craved a better, more sophisticated existence for years and had longed for all the things real money could buy. Now, here it was in front of her like a sickening cosmic joke.

"We should go to Bali." Zane's eyes were fixed on the money. "Rent one of those private villas on the beach."

Spider laughed. "Fuck Bali." He tossed a roll of cash in the air with one hand then caught it in the other. "I'm going to New York."

Amy was no longer listening to their chatter. Her attention was on the sounds coming from the street. Voices could be heard along with vehicle doors sliding open. She moved out of the kitchen leaving the two men to gloat over the cash.

Peering out of the front window, she saw the back end of an ambulance parked in the Foxhalls' driveway. Her heart did a weird slow flutter. Frank had returned home – home to find his wife dead on the kitchen floor. Her mind went to the blood spreading out like a ghoulish halo around Greta's head. Without thinking, Amy rushed to the front door and out onto the street.

There were paramedics and flashing lights. Standing on the footpath with a blanket draped over her shoulders, she watched the medics run a gurney out of the Foxhalls' house.

Noise, a clatter of movement, and voices fell away until all she saw was the trolley then Greta's face partially covered by an oxygen mask. Amy experienced a sensation of being outside herself as the world shrank to a pinpoint and only the gurney existed. Greta was alive! The relief hit Amy physically, enveloping all other senses.

She spotted Frank and the noises came rushing back. His face was devoid of colour as he spoke to the paramedic while watching his wife being lifted into the ambulance. Amy had done this to him – to them.

"Frank?" she called out.

When he turned, she expected to see recrimination in his eyes and instinctively she pulled the blanket over the scratches on her arm. The only thing visible in Frank's eyes was anguish. It made the large man look smaller.

Amy rushed toward him. "Is she…?" She didn't know how to finish the question.

Frank lifted a hand as though reaching for her. "She had a fall. She's unconscious." His voice was shaky. "I'll call you when I know what's happening."

Before Amy could reach him, he turned and followed his wife as she was rolled into the back of the ambulance. The doors slammed closed and a minute later the emergency vehicle backed out of the Foxhalls' driveway. Halfway down Cobblestone Lane, the siren burst to life and the ambulance sped off.

Amy stayed on the street even after the siren grew distant and eventually faded. When the lane settled into silence, she turned and re-entered the house.

"What's happening out there?" Zane asked, meeting her at the door. "Why are there sirens? What did the old guy say?"

"Greta's dead and Frank collapsed," she lied as she walked away leaving Zane tugging at his hair.

Chapter Twenty

"Hello, sweetheart." Her mother's voice, so comforting and familiar, brought tears to Amy's eyes.

She wanted nothing more than to be twelve again and on the couch snuggling up beside her mum, letting the woes of the world fly away and soaking in the comforting scent of Palmolive soap and peppermint tea. Listening to her mother's soothing voice. Back then it had been easier to dream of having a big future or have the childish illusion of someday owning a horse farm. Only now she had no future other than possibly a life in prison or living a life shadowed by guilt and fear.

"Mum," she started. "I…" *I've done something terrible.* The words were there, but she couldn't bring herself to speak them.

"Are you all right?" Her mother's voice sounded worried, yet alert.

Amy could almost see Catherine Holt bracing for bad news and at the same time ready to take action. She could always fix things. Make everything okay. But Greta was hurt and that couldn't be *fixed*. No amount of kind words could take that awful truth away.

"Is it him?" her mother asked lowering her voice. "Has he done something? Has he hurt you?"

"No." The denial came out too quickly. "Why would you ask that?"

There was silence on the line, save her mother's breathing.

"I don't understand any of this," Catherine burst out. "I don't know why you just packed up and left like that. None of it makes sense. Even before you left something wasn't right. You weren't yourself. Amy?"

"Stop, Mum." Amy closed her eyes. "I can't do this now."

"I'm sorry." Her mother sounded frightened. "Please, just talk to me. Whatever's happened, I can help."

Could she? Amy pressed the phone to her forehead. The temptation to let it all out tore at her, so much so that she almost missed the sound of a car pulling into the driveway.

"Amy?"

"Yes," Amy answered. "I'm just a bit homesick. You know, missing you and Darla."

"We miss you too." Catherine sounded relieved, but not convinced. "Why don't you come home this weekend? We could go to the farmer's market and then have lunch at Lacy's. The best gözleme in Perth. Your favourite, remember?"

Could she go home? Just get in her car and drive away from Cobblestone Lane? Leave Zane and Spider behind like a bad dream? She hadn't hurt anyone. None of what happened was her doing so why should she suffer? Why did her life have to be ruined?

It was a nice dream, but Amy knew it was just that: a dream. Life couldn't go back to normal, not now. She couldn't outrun what happened inside of the Foxhalls' kitchen.

"Not this weekend, but soon." The words came out as if from a stranger's mouth and as a flat certainty that she wouldn't be going home this weekend or any other. The realisation settled on her like a heavy blanket.

"I have to go." Amy was hurrying now, moving away from the lounge room and back to the bedroom.

She hung up while her mother was still speaking and shoved the phone in her pocket. Still dressed in the clothes she'd worn the day before, she closed the door and crawled into bed. If Zane came looking, she'd feign sleep.

It was kind of funny, she thought as she pulled the quilt up over her head. She'd spent the last year craving his attention like an addict.

Addict was the right word because like a junkie she'd been ready to beg, humiliate herself, and dump a young man's body or do anything for the high that came with Zane's love. She'd done whatever it took and now it was like the fever had broken. She'd detoxed and all she wanted now was to be left alone.

As it turned out, Zane didn't bother to check on her. The old Amy would have been crushed, sobbing like an abandoned dog until he found time to pat her on the head. All it had taken to set her free was almost ending her friend's life. The way he'd stared at Greta's body, in that moment she thought he was spellbound by the horror of watching the old lady bleed. Now she was sure he had deliberately averted his gaze while Spider squeezed Amy so hard that something inside her had cracked.

For a while she dozed, half aware of the voices coming from the other room. It was almost twenty-four hours since Greta was lifted into the ambulance. Greta was still alive. It was all Amy had left to cling to.

At some point she fell asleep and into the Foxhalls' kitchen where Greta was trying to flee. Only this time movements were slower. The light was crisp – sharper. Out of the corner of her eye, Amy saw movement. A hand shot out and hit Greta between the shoulders. The action was little more than a blur, overshadowed by watching Greta stumble forward. The sound of Greta's head hitting the island was like a clap of thunder. Amy woke with a start in almost complete darkness. Her phone was ringing. Not her mother as she'd expected but Frank.

"She's still in ICU." Frank sounded broken, far away and wrecked. "They said something about swelling on her brain. I don't know if she's going to…" He drew in a breath before continuing. "They said she might not regain consciousness."

"I can stay with her so you can come home and grab a few hours of sleep," Amy offered. Even in the fading light, she could see the scratches on her arm.

"You're a kind girl," he said. "Maybe later, but not now. I'll call you when I know more."

After hanging up, she made herself leave the bedroom. Only intending to drink a few handfuls from the tap and splash some water on her face, she made it halfway along the hall when she heard Spider's voice.

"We spend a couple of months in the US and then we'll have enough money to start our own operation."

"Maybe." Zane sounded unconvinced.

"We sell for ourselves. I've got some contacts in Perth," Spider continued. "It's easy money if we use the right people."

"I told you I'll think about it," Zane snapped.

They were talking about drugs. That didn't surprise her. Deep down she'd always known the job at the electrical store was a fantasy. What really shocked her was the way Zane spoke to Spider. All this time she'd thought Spider called the shots, but now it seemed Zane was in charge. Or was that how Spider played with him, letting him feel like he was making his own decisions?

"I have to decide what to do about Amy." Zane sounded matter of fact, as if discussing a minor detail.

"She'll keep her mouth shut." Spider was talking rapidly, trying to be reassuring. "And if she doesn't, she's the only one who the cops can place in that kitchen. She's the one who knew about the money."

"Let's hope that's enough," Zane replied.

They both still believed Greta was dead and Amy intended to keep it that way. She pressed herself against the wall. Had she misunderstood or was there menace in Zane's last few words? Either way she played no part in their future plans except as the fall guy. A week ago she'd thought she was in love with Zane. Now she realised she barely knew him. No. That was too easy. She knew what he was. She'd always known. It was easier to pretend because it made her feel less guilty about her obsession with him.

She heard movement. Murmured voices followed by rustling. Sounds that sent her scurrying back to the safety of the bedroom.

Back in bed, time passed without meaning. It seemed her life had narrowed to one room. Could it be a sign of things to come? She'd done little but sleep for what seemed like days yet still she drifted into slumber.

She awoke to daylight. Bathed in sweat, her mind ricocheted between the hand that hit Greta between the shoulder blades and the bag of money. No. Not the money but the photographs. Two separate things yet both important. Important how, she didn't yet know. But the need to know was like coming back to life after being in a coma.

There was silence in the house – the sort of hollow flat lack of sound that told her the place was empty. She'd been in the same clothes for two days, but showering would have to wait.

She needed to see those old photographs. With Zane and Spider gone, God knows where she intended to seize the opportunity. Feeling more focused than she had in days or perhaps months, she threw back the covers and leapt out of bed.

She began her search in the kitchen. A few minutes of opening and closing cupboards and she gave up and moved on to the lounge. Unsteady on her feet, she realised it had been almost two days since she'd last eaten.

There was a pizza box on the coffee table. The lingering smell of cheese and salami made her stomach groan with hunger. There were two slices left, cold and curled at the edges but that didn't stop her devouring them then licking the grease off her fingers.

Appetite sated, she checked under the couch but found nothing other than tumbleweed balls of dust and an empty pretzel packet. There were few hiding places left in the sparsely furnished room: the cupboard under the TV unit and a space behind the armchair. Holding her side as she moved, Amy made the rounds of the room and came up empty.

She'd barely left the master bedroom in days so it was unlikely the money was hidden there. The bathroom was little more than a box room with a sink and shower so that left the laundry room and spare bedroom. *Zane and Spider's room.* It was the first time she'd let herself even think the words. The idea of stepping into *their* room made her skin crawl.

Adjoining the kitchen, the laundry sat darkest of all the rooms in the house. It sat dank with dripping pipes and the ever-present smell of rust. For a moment she stood in the doorway unsure of what she really hoped to achieve. Were the photos important or just a way to distract her thoughts from the reality of her situation?

"I'm trapped. In danger. Facing prison." When she said this out loud it sounded impossible, but that didn't mean it wasn't true.

In the face of everything, a maddening certainty persisted, like an inkling she was missing something. Or perhaps fixating on a few old photos was a sign she was losing her mind?

"All right then." Almost absent-mindedly, she rubbed at her side.

Time was running out. Zane and Spider might be back any minute and she was taking too long.

She started with the linen cupboard. Aside from a few sheets and towels, the shelves were empty. Next, Amy checked the barrel of the old top loader washing machine. Finally, she turned to the broken-down dryer propped up on bricks in the far corner. Like the washing machine, the dryer was empty. Amy was ready to move on when she noticed the marks on the floor.

Surrounding the bricks that served as supports for the dryer were skids of grime. She touched her toe to one of the marks. It looked like the supports had been moved and then pushed back, but not all the way.

Shifting the dryer was easy enough if she did it slowly. A few short shoves and she managed to nudge the appliance away from the wall.

The backboard was loose. Two of the four screws that held it in place were only partially fastened. After a few twists of her fingers and a jab of pain in her ribs she managed to remove the loose screws. With the screws out, the board opened like a book cover and she spotted the carry-all.

Sunlight from the one small, slatted window in the room didn't quite reach the corner she stood in, but still she caught a glint of silver. It could have been dust, but Amy knew it was a spider's web. A sheen of sweat broke out across the back of her T-shirt.

Still crouched on the floor, Amy reached into the chasm and instantly felt the sticky silk touch of the web on her skin. Desperate to snatch back her arm, she grabbed the carry-all and pulled it out of its hiding place. Before opening the bag, she swatted at her arm while shuddering with disgust.

The cash was inside, still in rolls, but no longer in the canvas pouch. The photos were at the bottom of the bag. She lifted her shirt and shoved the pictures down her pants, not stopping to count them or even glance at the images before zipping up the carry-all and stuffing it back inside the wall.

Her fingers were damp with sweat, making replacing the screws difficult. With each second spent fiddling with the backboard, Amy expected to hear the slam of the front door or worse: Spider's voice behind her. Not daring to stop or look around, she pushed on until the backboard was back in place. A few seconds later, she shoved the dryer against the wall.

To her relief, the kitchen was empty and there was no sign of Spider's car on the driveway. Still, she felt the need to hurry. Rushing back to the bedroom, she grabbed some clean clothes and her phone before darting into the bathroom.

With the door locked, she sat on the floor and pulled the photos out of her jeans. There were three in total, all of them black and white snaps. Until now she wasn't sure what it was that puzzled her about the photos. Now she realised it was Greta's image in one of the photos that caught her attention.

In the photo, Greta was much younger, perhaps in her early twenties and dressed in a wedding gown. Greta's striking features were unmistakable, even in profile. Her hair was pulled away from her face, held in place by a crown of tiny white flowers. Although she'd only known Greta with white hair and the colour wasn't apparent in the photo, Amy was sure the young woman's hair was strawberry blonde.

She touched the image of Greta's young face. It wasn't the novelty of seeing her friend as a beautiful young woman that puzzled Amy. It was the sorrowful expression on her face as she looked away from the camera. Beside her was a young man roughly handsome with the beginnings of a receding hairline that beamed with pleasure. His hand not holding Greta's, but clamped over it. Undoubtedly, the groom and definitely not Frank.

Amy tried to remember the array of photos on the Foxhalls' piano. Black and white images, some of Greta as a child. Other frames held photos of elderly couples. One showed a man riding a black horse. No wedding photos.

She held the picture so the light from the bathroom window fell on Greta's face. It was odd that there were no wedding photos in the couple's house. In fact, Amy couldn't recall any pictures of Frank and Greta together. Maybe that was why this picture had caught her attention.

The other two photos were both of the man Amy now thought of as the groom. In one of them he stood with a plump older woman. In the other he leaned against an old Holden EH with a cigarette clamped between his lips and grinning, but somehow the smile looked cruel. The final photo showed the groom as a teenager alongside a little boy.

Amy turned the photo over. Written on the back in clumsy letters were three words: *Ron and Frank*. Staring at the writing, the world seemed to tilt and she felt as though she'd fallen into an episode of "The Twilight Zone." She could almost hear the host's voice as he introduced the show. Same name, same bride, different face.

Without thinking, Amy rubbed at her birthmark. What did it mean? Why were these photos with the money? The other day she'd been too enveloped in shock to put things together, but now she wondered why the bag that contained fifteen thousand dollars less than a week ago now contained almost five times that amount and a photo of Greta marrying another man. Not just that, but photos of Frank, only not the Frank whom Amy knew.

She shuffled the photos together. Whatever secrets Frank and Greta were keeping didn't change what happened, but it was something to occupy her thoughts. Enough to distract her from the horror show that kept running in her mind if only for a short time. It couldn't block out what she'd seen in the Foxhalls' kitchen, but it was something.

She hid the photos and took a shower. Under the hot jet she felt some of the dirt wash away. Some semblance of balance returned to her thoughts. She'd wait until Greta recovered, she thought, not wanting to imagine the alternative. Zane and Spider still thought Greta was dead and Amy intended to keep it that way because if the two men knew the truth they might panic. She'd seen what they were capable of. God knows what they'd do if their backs were against the wall.

If Greta remembered what happened, then Amy would go to the police and tell them everything. Zane and Spider would have to face what they'd done. It wasn't much of a plan, but it would have to do for now.

Chapter Twenty-one

A parcel sat on the veranda. Not surprisingly he'd overlooked it the other day. Picking up the package and seeing Greta's name on it was like a fresh stab of pain. For a while Frank just held the package trying to picture her with her glasses perched on her nose while placing an online order.

The image, while comforting, also hurt. Not because she was gone, although that was a well of sorrow so deep he feared there *was* no bottom, but because the parcel was a part of her. A part of her thoughts and actions. The last thing she'd ordered. Something that meant enough to her that she had to have it.

She's gone. The words reverberated in his mind. Shock, heart failure, the doctors threw terms at him as if they had meaning when the only meaningful thing in his world was over.

Frank let himself in the house, still holding the package. Muscle memory moved him with no real thought or purpose. Close the front door, keys in the bowl on the hall stand, then take the parcel to the kitchen.

No, not the kitchen. He couldn't face that room, not yet. Instead, he went to the sitting room and sank into the armchair. He set the parcel down on the side table, handling it as though it was as fragile as a sparrow's egg.

His body ached with weariness. People talked about hurting, wrote songs about it, and poetry comparing loss to the splitting of one's heart. He felt none of those things, only fear. The world and everything in it was harsh and foreign now and he was lost. That was the simplicity of loss.

His phone rang, its shrill the only sound in the empty house. Without bothering to answer, he pulled the phone out of his jacket and dismissed the call. He wanted oblivion, but for now sleep would have to do.

Upstairs, he peeled off his jacket and kicked off his shoes then fell into bed. Her scent was on the sheets, sweet and delicate. Closing his eyes, he imagined her there beside him before sleep came as a merciful blackout.

"That tree needs pruning, the branches are blocking out the light," Greta said shaking the colander. "Just the low branches though, don't go getting the ladder out."

She was at the sink washing apricots, examining each piece of fruit before setting it on the chopping board. When she picked up the knife and started chopping, the blade looked disproportionally large in her hand. Frank wanted to warn her to use a smaller knife but for some reason he was sobbing.

"It's all right, darling." There was music and kindness in her voice while she chopped with furious speed. "Once I make the tart we'll be free."

He started to speak, but realised the apricots were rolling off the chopping board and bouncing across the kitchen floor, tumbling through a pool of dark liquid.

"Greta, don't you see?" His voice was lost to the sound of the knife striking the board and the fruit pounding the floor.

Frank opened his eyes. His phone was ringing from the end of the bed where he'd tossed his jacket. Ignoring the call, he scrubbed a hand over his face trying to rub away the remnants of the dream.

When the phone stopped, he forced himself to sit up. He didn't know which was worse, the drilling shriek of the phone or the sudden total silence that had no trace of her presence. Judging by the light, it was early evening.

The numbness was ebbing, but the fear was paralysing. Fear of pain. Fear of loneliness. Fear of the rage and heartache that was building in him like an explosion. Their time together was coming to an end. They'd both known it was, but not like this. Not his Greta. The urge to fall back onto the pillow and sob was almost irresistible, but Frank pushed himself to keep going.

He was barely out of bed when the pounding started. Someone was at the door. The idea of conversing with someone seemed alien and at the same time he wanted something to fill the silence.

"Mr Foxhall, I heard about your wife." For the first time since Frank met the detective, he looked unsure of himself. "I just thought I'd check in, see how you're doing."

Frank held the door, not wanting to invite the cop inside. "I was sleeping."

Worsten nodded. "Yeah, of course. Sorry if I woke you. Just with your brother and everything I thought I'd stop by."

Worsten seemed genuine, but Frank didn't know him well enough to be sure. He also didn't have the strength to find out. Besides, if he'd been at home with Greta instead of at the station answering the man's questions, she'd still be alive.

"I really don't feel up to talking," Frank said. "Thanks for stopping by."

He closed the door in the cop's face, not giving him time to respond. Would the detective think his reaction was suspicious? Worsten said he'd heard about what had happened to Greta, yet there was no way the cop could have known about the accident unless he'd been keeping tabs on Frank. What did it matter? In a few days he'd bury Greta and then he didn't care what happened.

Still unable to face the kitchen, he went to the sitting room and poured himself a generous measure of whiskey. He'd never been much of a drinker, but with the pain under his ribs twisting like a knife, now was as good a time to start as any. As the room sank into darkness he switched on the side lamp and took up his position in the armchair.

Three months ago, when tests confirmed he had cancer, he'd refused treatment. With Greta's condition worsening he couldn't risk being too sick to care for her. At his GP's insistence, Frank agreed to take pain relief, heavy duty stuff that remained unopened in the bathroom cabinet.

A few handfuls of pills washed down with a couple of whiskey chasers and all the pain and grief would be over. He didn't believe in an afterlife. In light of what he'd done to Ron, Frank now prayed there was nothing waiting for him on the other side. At this point he'd embrace the black finality of death. Nothingness with Greta was better than the whole world without her.

On an empty stomach, the liquor soon took effect. When he rose and poured himself another, the floor moved under his feet and his head swam. Lurching back to the chair, his thoughts returned to Greta's last moments. Holding her hand. Watching the rise and fall of her chest. With the memory came tears. Nothing he'd seen or done in his life came close to the anguish of watching her depart. Head in hands, sobs wracked his body as he recalled the few moments when she regained consciousness.

Who are you? What are you doing here? There was fear in her voice. Her beautiful eyes wide, pleading with him.

Their last seconds together and she didn't know him. Greta's hand gripped his, her fingers warm and alive as she repeated the words a second time. A few seconds later, she was gone.

He drained the glass and leaned back in the chair. Unused to the liquor, his thoughts were growing hazy and his limbs numb; a feeling he thought he could get used to.

* * *

Morning came. His first without her. Stiff from a night in the chair, he shuffled upstairs.

There were preparations to make. Calls to be placed. Greta was waiting. He didn't want to think about her alone and amongst strangers. Last night he'd wallowed. Today he would do what was necessary.

Hot water helped. Standing under the shower, his mind began to clear before the effects of the night kicked in and he vomited over the drainpipe. As he watched the meagre contents of his stomach wash away and the smell of regurgitated whiskey fill his nose, his stomach lurched a second time.

He leaned a shoulder against the wall as the water washed over his face. This wasn't him. This wasn't the man Greta loved. He allowed himself another minute under the shower before drying off, cleaning his teeth, and shaving.

His phone was ringing again. This time he picked it up and saw three missed calls from Amy.

"Damn." He'd promised to call her.

Breaking the news to his neighbour would mean speaking the words and reliving the worst moment of his life and most likely him breaking down in front of the young woman. Saying it out loud would make it real – final. No matter how selfish, he wasn't ready so he tossed the phone on the bed. Just a few more hours alone with his grief. Enough time to gather the strength to put his loss into words.

When he reached the stairs, someone knocked the front door. Cursing Worsten under his breath, he descended the staircase.

"Frank?" Amy stood on the doorstep, her young face fearful and drawn.

The words wouldn't come. If he'd had any notion of what to say, it escaped him and all he could muster was a shake of his head.

"Oh no." Amy's expression changed from concern to horror as her hands flew to her face.

He should have said something. Some words of solace, but watching her distress he felt helpless and, in some way, grateful. Grateful that Amy shared his grief. She was so young and alive. When she wrapped her arms around him, he wept on her shoulder.

Chapter Twenty-Two

She expected everything to be as it was when Greta was on the kitchen floor. Amy pictured a pool of blood littered with apricots and shards of smashed china. All just as it was, minus Greta's body. A reality to match the image now seared into her memory.

The debris of that horrific morning was still present, but not as she remembered. Wheel marks in blood now turning brown criss-crossed the floorboards. The shattered mess of the bowl and fruit had been swept aside, replaced by discarded medical packets. A lone piece of clear tubing stuck to a glob of semi-dried blood. All the evidence of a desperate battle to save a woman's life.

This was the mess Frank couldn't face – a mess Amy had volunteered to clean. It was almost comical that she thought by scrubbing the floor she could wash away what she'd allowed to happen. And then there was Frank's tearful gratitude. His kind words were like a rusty nail in her heart.

Despite the heat outside, Amy was cold and shivered as she picked her way around the room to the cupboard that contained the cleaning products. Almost in a trance, she pushed up her sleeves and started sweeping and scrubbing, biting back nausea as the smell of blood mixed with soap coated the inside of her mouth.

This, she told herself, was what she deserved. No, a fraction of what she should feel for the damage she'd caused. For her lies and selfishness. Even her tears were an affront to Frank's grief. She'd listened to him sob all the while wondering if he knew about the missing money. And if he did, would he suspect her? Would he involve the police?

Amy picked up the bucket. The floor was cleaner. The water in the bucket now mingled with blood had turned into a muddy mixture. A sickening brew which she poured into the sink then washed away.

While Greta was alive, Amy had clung to a glimmer of hope. Greta would be able to vouch for her. There was a chance she could make Frank and the police understand what really happened. But when Frank answered the door and shook his head, all hope died.

Now he was upstairs picking out a dress, the clothing Greta would wear when she was cremated. In the midst of her misery, Amy's mind went back to the photographs she'd retrieved from the carry-all.

Thinking of the pictures sparked a memory: Greta referring to Frank as *that man of mine*. Amy swiped away a strand of hair that was plastered to her forehead as she opened the cupboard and returned the bucket to it storage place. She recalled numerous times when Greta spoke of Frank in that way. Not my husband, but that man of mine. Then there was the picture of Ron and Frank – a different Frank. A picture she'd found only days after Ron was murdered.

Amy shook her head and stowed the dustpan and brush alongside the bucket. Why was it that her guilty mind kept distracting her by obsessing over the photographs?

"You're finished." Frank's voice made her jump.

Amy closed the cupboard and turned to face him. "Yes, I'll fix you something to eat and then–"

"No," Frank said from the doorway. "You've done enough. You should go now."

He was staring at her, his eyes shiny with tears. Was it grief or was there something else? Suspicion? No, it wasn't possible. Only half an hour ago he'd welcomed her in and accepted her help. He was still in shock. Was it any wonder his emotions were all over the place?

"Sorry," Amy said, wiping her hands on her jeans. "I'll let you rest."

When she moved to exit the kitchen, Frank remained in the doorway. There was an awkward second when it appeared he wasn't going to move. Amy thought she could hear her own heartbeat and wondered if it was so loud that Frank could hear it too.

"I'll get going then," she tried again.

To her relief, he stepped aside. As she passed, Frank moved with unexpected speed and grabbed her wrist.

"What happened?" he asked staring at her forearm.

Her mind raced. His hand, impossibly large, held firm. Why hadn't she remembered to roll down her sleeves after she finished cleaning? Or more importantly, why hadn't she thought of a cover story to excuse the scratches?

Her mouth was dry, making speaking difficult. "I hurt myself on one of the cages at work."

He nodded but continued to stare at the scratches. Unable to stand his scrutiny a second longer, Amy yanked her arm free.

"Call me if you need anything," she muttered, already on her way to the front door.

The hallway seemed longer, stretching like something in a nightmare. When she reached the front door, she half expected Frank to be on her heels barring her exit. Mercifully, she made it out of the house without further incident. When she hit the garden path, she picked up speed.

Once inside her own house, she paced the living room. Frank knew. Why else would he have questioned her about the scratches? Was she paranoid? Maybe he hadn't figured it all out, but he wasn't a stupid man. It was only a matter of time.

Panicked, she raced to the bedroom and grabbed her suitcase from under the bed. She opened cupboards and drawers, tossing clothing into the case while trying to formulate a plan. Leave Bunbury. Not home, too obvious. Somewhere else. Anywhere as long as it was far away.

"What are you doing?" How had she not heard Zane enter the house? Or maybe he'd been here all along.

"He knows," she said, still packing. "I can't stay here. Greta's dead and Frank knows something."

"What do you mean? Greta's dead. Of course she's dead," Zane persisted, grabbing her arm. "What's going on?"

Amy winced internally. How could she forget she'd lied about Greta's condition? What hope would she have if Frank went to the police when she couldn't keep one lie straight in her mind? It was all piling up, filling her thoughts, and at the forefront the way Frank looked at her when he asked about the scratches.

"I don't know. I just can't do this anymore." She pulled away from him. "I can't stay here."

Zane sniffed. "Where will you go? You don't even have a passport."

"But you do," she said dropping the pile of clothing she had in her hands. "You and Spider have it all worked out, but what about me?"

Anger swelled inside her. Zane and Spider had the money. They had an exit plan that didn't include her. If she didn't do something, she'd be the one left to face the consequences of what they'd done.

"Maybe I should just go to the police," Amy said, facing him.

It was a stupid threat, one made out of anger. The moment the words left her mouth she knew she'd gone too far. He moved with swiftness, spinning her around and forcing her against the wall. She gasped at the stab of pain in her ribs as her back made contact with the plaster.

"You're not going to the cops." His face was only centimetres from hers. "Get that idea out of your brain." He shook her so her head hit the wall. "This is a chance for me to get out of this shit town. I'm not going to let you screw it up for me."

The back of Amy's skull burned with pain. He'd shouted at her, kicked furniture over, but this was the first time he deliberately hurt her. The sudden violence was like the hammering of the final nail in the coffin that was their relationship. Instead of heartache, all she felt was fear and anger. Fear over what he might do to her and anger because she'd let him bring her so low. Because *she* had allowed it.

Still squeezing her shoulders, he shoved her towards the bed. When he let go of her, Amy stumbled, catching herself before hitting the floor.

"Find out what he knows," Zane said, speaking each word with venom.

What he was asking was insane, but she didn't dare argue. All she could do was marvel at how blind and stupid she'd been. This wasn't love. It was bondage. A sick and destructive circle where she'd been a willing participant. And all the while there had been a part of her that loved the excitement of being with a man like him. Not caring what damage she caused as long as she had Zane. Now she realised she'd never had him, not in any meaningful way.

"Okay," she said, rubbing the back of her head and not bothering to wipe at the tears that were now streaming down her cheeks. "I'll talk to Frank and see what I can find out."

She had no intention of doing what he wanted, but agreeing was the safest course of action. She'd been afraid of Spider and then Frank, but the real danger was closer to home. It had always been beside her.

Watching Zane roll his shoulders, shrugging off what he'd just done to her, Amy thought of that moment in the Foxhalls' kitchen when she saw a hand shoot out. A hand that thumped between Greta's shoulders as she was trying to run. Zane's hand. It was Zane who pushed Greta into the marble countertop.

Chapter Twenty-three

He'd meant to open Greta's wardrobe and pick out her favourite dress. Something simple and elegant. But when he glanced at the nightstand and saw her book, the strength left his body.

First running his fingers over the cover, Frank held the novel between his hands. He tried to recall the last time he'd watched her reading and despite every miserable second of the last few days he found himself smiling.

Greta loved reading. Books were so much a part of who she was. Her stellar mind always sought knowledge, insight, and enlightenment. It occurred to him that her reading glasses should be with her when they said goodbye. It was a thought that brought him both comfort and sorrow.

She kept a pair of spectacles in the nightstand as well as hand cream scented with juniper berries. Yet, when he opened the drawer, the glasses were nowhere in sight. It was a small thing; missing reading glasses, but suddenly the most pressing.

He set the book down and scanned the room. He could hear Amy downstairs and for a second his mind tricked him into thinking it was Greta. The running water and cupboards opening and normal sounds, in the blink of an eye reality kicked in with all its glaring lights and harsh edges. It crushed his momentary calm.

The glasses. Frank let out a tired breath and sunk to one knee. Flipping up the quilt, he peered under the bed. Just as he'd thought, the spectacles had fallen off the nightstand perhaps when Greta set them on top of the book or maybe she'd knocked them off when she was applying her hand cream.

Either way, there they were, delicate tortoise-shell frames sitting on the floor amongst the dust balls. He scooped the glasses up and realised something was out of place. Frank frowned, confused not by what he saw but by what was missing. The bag was gone.

He remained on his knee, gazing at the empty patch of floor. A moment ago his mind was filled with memories of juniper berries and reading glasses. Now his thoughts turned cold.

The money was gone. No, not gone. Taken. Barely noticing the bone on bone grind of his kneecap, he sprung up and searched the room. He had to be sure. Any small doubt that Greta might have moved the bag and forgot to tell him evaporated when his systematic search turned up nothing.

Finally, he stopped and sat on the bed. Greta in a pool of blood and almost a hundred thousand dollars gone. He'd been so sure her fall had been an accident, but the missing money changed everything. It didn't make sense, yet it made perfect sense. Someone had come into the house, attacked Greta then taken the money.

He ran a hand over his bristly pate. He felt like he was losing his mind. No one knew about the money, yet it wasn't a random burglary because nothing else had been touched. But no one knew. His mind ran in circles, always coming back to that certainty. There were only three people that knew about the cash: himself, Greta, and Ron.

Even if Ron had blabbed to his neighbour, there was no way the man would have known exactly where to look.

Still trying to piece everything together, Frank heard the tap running in the kitchen. *Amy*. Her name popped in his mind like a gunshot. She was the only other person who had been in the house, the only person Greta talked to. With her confusion growing, it was possible that Greta had let something slip. What's more, on the day he found Greta on the floor there had been no sign of forced entry. Greta would have let Amy in because she trusted her without question and so had he until now.

Was he jumping too far with his conclusions? Even if Amy was a thief, he found it hard to believe she was a killer. He'd thought her a gentle person. A bit shy and nervous, but not the violent type.

In the end, it was the scratches that convinced him. That and the terrified look in her eyes when he'd asked about them. She was guilty. Seeing it written all over her face, it took every ounce of willpower he possessed not to wring the truth out of her.

In the silence, Frank poured himself a drink. He put on a record, something slow and moody: the French version of *The Windmills of Your Mind* by Charles Aznavour. A song they used to dance to, holding each other and swaying in time with the music.

His dancing days were over. Now, he simply sat in his armchair as Aznavour's soulful voice filled the house. He thought about the police, but that would only complicate matters. Worsten would have questions about the money. About the photographs. Questions that would lead to Frank's arrest. Time he couldn't afford to waste.

Greta still needed him to finish things. He'd say goodbye to her as planned. But for now, nothingness would have to wait. At least until he gave Greta justice.

He took another sip of whiskey relishing the numbness it brought. Tomorrow he'd get to the truth of what happened. But even as he thought about Amy and what he must do, his resolve wavered. His anger also wavered. His chest constricted as if someone had thrown a thick belt over him and pulled it tight. Frank gasped and pressed his fist to his bicep. The tightness eased and he let out a long breath.

He'd never hurt a woman before and despite everything he still felt affection for the girl. Affection now tainted with rage. He held up the glass wondering how much he needed to drink before he had the stomach to get his revenge.

Chapter Twenty-four

She felt like a rag doll, bruised and battered: tossed around by unfeeling hands. There was a golf ball sized knot on the back of her head. Her shoulders ached and her ribs were purple with bruises. It seemed violence was her life now. The physical pain was one thing, but the constant fear was worse. For the first time in her life she understood how battered women can become, if not accustomed to, resigned to how they were treated. No, that wasn't right. No one can be resigned to abuse.

She'd finished packing, but it was clear Zane wouldn't let her go. Over the last three days there had been a shift in the dynamics of the house. The atmosphere had morphed into something unhealthy. *Had it ever been otherwise?* It was no longer Zane and Amy with Spider always creeping around. Now it was Spider and Zane and she the outsider, an unwelcome guest in what was supposed to be her home. A home that felt unsafe and far from hospitable.

"What does he know?" Spider wasn't lounging now. He was edgy and moving around the kitchen in sharp jolting steps.

"I don't know." Amy had lost count of how many times they'd asked this same question.

"We can be out of here by the day after tomorrow, sooner if we just hide out somewhere until the flight." Spider was still talking, but now his attention was on Zane. "He hasn't gone to the police so he *must* have something to hide."

Amy had been sitting at the kitchen table and now dropped her head into her hands. How much more of this could she take before she turned into a screaming mess?

"What if old mate decided to end it all?" Spider continued. "There'd be no one to go to the police. No one to ask questions about missing money. It wouldn't matter what he thought he knew."

Amy looked from Spider to Zane and watched him sip his coffee. She couldn't believe what she was hearing. Was she crazy or were they calmly discussing murder?

She dropped her hands onto the table. "Haven't you done enough?" As hard as she tried, it was impossible to keep the exasperation out of her voice.

"Just think about it?" Zane insisted, standing over her. "We'd be in the clear – free to do whatever we wanted without having to worry about the old guy going to the cops."

"He's not going to the cops," Amy said, trying to stay calm. "If he *was* going to, he'd have done it by now."

Zane shook his head. "You can't be sure of that. None of us can. I don't want to spend the next five or ten years wondering when Frank will change his mind. He's the only one that knows a crime was committed. It ends with him."

Amy thought of the photos. She knew Frank and Greta had plenty to hide, but she wasn't about to share the information with Zane or Spider. Nor would she sit back and let them hurt Frank. She'd let too much happen already. It was time to stop them before anyone else was injured.

"You're right." Her response caught them off guard. "But just let me talk to him. You wanted me to find out what he knows," she said addressing Zane.

Spider stopped pacing and watched her. There was distaste in his gaze. Lip curled and head cocked, he might as well have been watching a blow fly crawl over his dinner. Zane on the other hand was listening intently.

She was halfway there. She had Zane's attention. Now all she had to do was play on their greed.

"Frank told me they owned number four and two. That hundred grand is small change to him. I think there's more." She glanced at Spider and just as she'd hoped, his eyes were alight. "He's old, grieving. Just let me talk to him."

* * *

She had no clear plan in mind, but at least she'd stalled Zane and Spider. She wished for time to think, but she'd have to come up with something fast because she was approaching the Foxhalls' front door.

There were few lights on inside the house. When Frank answered, the hall was in darkness, making it impossible to see his face. Even in the gloom she could make out his shape, large and unyielding.

"What is it?" There was brusqueness in his tone as he barred her entrance.

Determined not to be put off, Amy pushed on. "I need to talk to you, please."

He didn't respond straight away. Behind him, music drifted down the hall, deep and sorrowful. An unfamiliar melody and lyrics in another language, the song beautiful and heartbreaking.

"Did you do it?" His voice caught on the last word. "Did you hurt her?"

She'd prepared for this, but still the directness of the question took her by surprise. There was so much she wanted to say.

"No," Amy said. "I didn't."

She waited, bracing herself for what would come next. The door slammed in her face? Angry recriminations or worse? Without being able to see his eyes, she had no idea if he believed her.

"Come in," he said and stepped aside.

Frank turned off the music and slumped into the armchair. He'd been drinking. She could smell the whiskey. Amy watched as he picked up a glass and took a swallow. He didn't ask her to sit, but she did so anyway, taking a position on the sofa so she faced him.

The explanations she'd rehearsed, the words that made sense in her mind, were eaten up by nerves and guilt. What could she say that would make him understand why Greta was dead? How could she ask him not to hate her when she hated herself?

"I found the money when I was using the bathroom." It wasn't how she planned to begin, but it seemed like as good a place as any. "I only meant to look at your bedroom and…" Amy paused and pressed her fingers to her eyes. "I stumbled across the bag."

When he looked at her, Frank's face was stony. "So, you came back when I wasn't here and took it?"

"No. No, that's not what happened," she said holding up her hands. "It wasn't like that at all."

Amy started talking, beginning with how she'd told Zane about the money. Then she moved on to the morning Greta showed up at her door confused looking for someone named Jim and insisting Amy take her to see her father. When Amy got to the part about the kitchen and Greta hitting her head, Frank shifted in his chair. It was the first time he'd moved since she started telling the story.

"I tried to stop them," Amy said, leaning forward. "I wanted to call an ambulance, but they wouldn't let me." She could hear herself and how pathetic the excuses sounded.

"But you didn't call for help," Frank said setting his glass down. "You left her to die on the floor alone."

"Yes." The word was a whisper. Amy could see the moment in her mind's eye. Greta face down, the blood blossoming around her white hair. "I didn't want the money. She was my friend."

Frank slapped his palm on the arm of the chair and Amy jumped. "You left her to die," he repeated with more ferocity this time.

"Please, you need to understand." Desperate, Amy pulled up her T-shirt revealing the purple and yellow bruises covering her ribs. "I tried."

He hissed out a shocked breath and ran a hand over his head.

"I told Zane about the money," Amy continued. "But I never wanted any of this. I never wanted anyone to get hurt. I cared for Greta. You have to believe me."

She realised she was still holding the T-shirt up and quickly pulled it down.

"You've had days. Why didn't you go to the police?" Frank asked. "They did that to you." He waved a hand in her direction. "Why protect them?"

"I'm not protecting them," Amy said. "The scratches on my arm, the ones Greta did when we were in the car, Spider said it would look like I was responsible. The police would find my skin under Greta's nails and I'd go to prison." Frank looked unconvinced so she tried again. "They were going to blame the whole thing on me. I didn't know what to do."

Frank got up and poured himself another drink. He held the bottle up to her, but Amy shook her head. She wasn't sure how she'd expected this to go, but at least he wasn't attacking her, not yet.

"What I don't understand," Frank began as he sat back in his chair, "is why they haven't run. How are they so sure I won't realise the money is missing and go to the police?"

Amy explained that Zane and Spider thought that by having that much money in the house Frank must have something to hide and, if the cops showed up, they intended to blame it on her.

"They're right though, aren't they?" Amy questioned. "You do have something to hide."

Frank regarded her over the top of his glass. Judging by the redness in his eyes, he was well on his way to being drunk.

"I saw the photos," she added. "You're not Frank Foxhall, are you?"

He held up a hand, signalling her to stop. "I'm tired, Amy. You can ask your questions tomorrow."

He was dismissing her. Amy's stomach flipped at the thought of returning home. Now it was out, or at least most of what happened. The idea of being back in the house with Zane and Spider made her skin crawl with fear. Fear for herself and for what they might do to Frank.

"There are things I need to tell you." Amy leaned forward frantic to make him understand. "Things you need to know."

"You'll stay here tonight," he said, as if he'd read her thoughts. "The spare room's upstairs on the right. Use your phone. Tell them I'm drunk." He gave a dry laugh. "It's half true. Say you're keeping an eye on me. Make them believe I don't know the money is missing."

He was on his feet, his gait slightly unsteady as he headed towards the hall. "You're a smart girl. You'll think of something."

She opened her mouth to protest, but he cut her off.

"Tomorrow," he said, without turning around. "Tell me tomorrow."

Amy remained in the sitting room listening to Frank climb the stairs. A moment later a door closed and the house fell silent.

She considered slipping out of the house and returning home, but facing the two men was more than she could bear. Instead, she did as Frank had instructed and pulled out her phone.

He doesn't know! He's drunk so I'm staying the night to keep an eye on him.

When texting Zane, she usually included kisses. Now it was difficult to recall feeling so in love with him. How could she have been so desperate for his attention and affection? And how could the memory of that longing still be there, but now more like an old wound that had healed and had left a scar in its wake? She sent the text knowing he wouldn't care what she was doing as long as he was in the clear and the money remained in his possession.

While she had the phone out, Amy noticed a missed call from her mother. She thought about their conversation the day before and could only imagine the worry she had caused.

Fingers hovering over the keypad, she considered calling. It was only eight o'clock. Her mother would be awake, probably reading or watching the late news. As much as Amy wanted to hear her mother's voice and alleviate some of the worry, she couldn't bring herself to place the call. Instead, she fired off a text, hoping it would help in some way to put her mother's mind at rest.

Everything's fine. I'll be home for a visit soon. Love you. X

It wasn't much, but it might buy her some time. Time to do what she wasn't quite sure, and right now she was too exhausted to think about it any further. She'd slept so much yet it wasn't enough. There was more she needed to tell Frank. Most importantly, he needed to know he was in danger. And then there was the truth about Greta's accident. The truth being it was no accident. But Frank was right. It could wait until tomorrow. It would have to.

Instead of the spare room, she kicked off her shoes and grabbed a throw rug from the end of the sofa. After days of unending fear and guilt, being in the Foxhalls' house under Frank's roof she felt safe. Amy pulled the rug up and turned off the lamp. In minutes, she was asleep.

Chapter Twenty-five

"Where are we going?" Amy had to hurry to keep pace. "What does this have to do with the photos?"

Frank was a few steps ahead of her, moving along the track in a way that belied his age. Long graceful strides, an almost casual pace for him, but one she had to use a lot of energy to match. They were on a trail that Amy had no idea existed until this morning.

"You wanted to know about Frank Foxhall. It's easier to show you." He'd spoken over his shoulder without slowing.

She thought of stopping, refusing to move until he explained where they were going, but she had a feeling it was wiser to follow and ask questions later. Since she woke less than half an hour ago to find a cup of coffee waiting for her on the side table and Frank back in his spot in the armchair, there had been little in the way of conversation.

They drank their coffee in silence – a silence only broken when she mentioned the night before. Minutes later, she was pulling on her shoes and following him through the back gate.

It was a little past seven o'clock, too early for the sun to have much bite, but warm enough for perspiration to break out on the back of her neck. Watching Frank's back, she could see a damp line forming between his shoulders – shoulders so broad that they filled the narrow path.

They were at least a kilometre from the house and surrounded by dense bush. It occurred to her that after admitting she was involved in his wife's death, following him into such an isolated area was at best foolhardy.

"Frank?" This time she did stop, clamping a hand to her aching ribs. "Slow down."

"Not much further," he said, swatting a branch out of the way.

A moment later, he veered left and disappeared into the trees. Amy hesitated. Her heart hammered and not just from the effort of keeping up. She was nervous. Glancing back the way they'd come, she saw nothing but dense growth and foliage that leaned in and surrounded her on all sides.

"Amy?" His voice came from a tangle of trees, beckoning her to follow.

Still wavering, her thoughts were racing. *Follow or run?* Run where and back to what? She wanted to trust Frank. Her instincts told her he was a good man, but everything she thought she knew about him was a lie.

But who was she to judge? Her whole life was a series of lies. Hers, Zane's and now Frank's. Amy looked up at the sky flawlessly blue and unmarred by clouds. She wanted to believe that nothing ugly could happen under such a perfect firmament.

"Amy?" he called again, his voice further away.

If he wanted to hurt her, he could have done so last night or this morning or during all the hours they'd been alone together. But above all was curiosity. She wanted to know the truth about Frank Foxhall. In the midst of all the chaos and uncertainty, it was gnawing curiosity that drove her off the track and into the trees.

She found him in a small clearing, a spot where sunlight lit up the bush grass turning it from green to silver.

"There." He pointed to a cluster of grass trees. "He's been here for fifteen years."

Thinking she was missing something, Amy looked around.

"We put him there together, Greta and me," Frank said, still staring at the trees.

It suddenly became clear and she understood what she was looking at. Not the grass trees, but a burial site. This was the secret the Foxhalls had been keeping.

"You mean you buried a body here?" Amy asked.

Frank nodded. "I started all this. A stupid kid going off to a war he barely understood. I told her not to wait for me and so she ended up with him." There was bitterness in his voice, but mostly sorrow. "If I'd known she was carrying my baby, things would have been different. Or if I'd just realised that there would never be anyone else like her. But when you're that young it's hard to imagine not being happy. It's almost impossible to tell the young to tread carefully."

Amy understood he was talking about Greta and the man in the wedding photo: the real Frank Foxhall. She had questions but thought it better to let him tell it in his own way.

"I came home from Vietnam to find my mother had passed and Greta had married and moved away." He hooked his hands on his hips, still staring at the spot where the body was buried. "So many lost years. I moved from place to place. There were women, but nothing ever came close to how it was with Greta. That sort of loneliness is not something easily explained."

Listening to his story was painful. At times Amy had to fight back tears, especially as Frank talked about trying to find purpose. He spoke of a nomadic existence that paled in comparison to what Greta suffered at the hands of the real Frank. A gambler and womaniser, violent and cruel, he'd delivered a savage beating that sent Greta into early labour. She gave birth to a baby girl who lived a few brief weeks. At some point Frank sat on a fallen log where Amy joined him.

"Why did she stay?" As soon as the words were out, she realised how hypocritical she sounded. She'd willingly stayed in a destructive relationship.

"Why?" Frank repeated without a trace of scorn or judgement. "The baby at first. Then embarrassment, I think. Not wanting to return home and face the questions. From what Greta told me, Frank Foxhall promised to change and for a while he did. He stopped drinking and found a job. Things got better and then worse. At one point he was in an institution. Greta would have felt duty-bound to stay and care for him. She didn't take her vows lightly. Not that the rat bastard deserved her care," Frank added with rancour that surprised her.

"When she tried to leave, he threatened to hurt himself. By the time they returned to Bunbury he'd gambled away whatever money Greta had left. It was only because her father left her the house and the other properties on the lane that she was saved from poverty."

When Frank continued, he sounded more tired than bitter. "That's the long answer. The short one is life is complicated." He gave a dry laugh.

"Something brought me back here," he continued. "If I believed in such things, I'd say Greta's sadness had called out to me." He scrubbed a hand over his head. "We ran into each other by chance, me and Greta, and it was like nothing had changed. For me it felt like walking into the sunlight after years of winter. We started seeing each other. She was married, but I felt no guilt. It was right. It felt right." He stressed the last word. "We were planning on going away together." He shrugged. "Europe. Maybe France. Then one night she rang me. She said Frank knew about us. I could barely understand what she was saying."

He stopped talking and closed his eyes. Amy watched his profile. He looked like a man preparing for pain.

"When I got to the house, it was too late. Blood was everywhere," he continued. "He, Frank, tried to stab her. They struggled and she killed him."

Amy thought she knew where the story was heading, but had never imagined Greta capable of violence. It was almost too much to process.

"It was self-defence," he said, turning to look at Amy again. "Greta was in shock, badly beaten and terrified. I spent half the night just holding her. Back then the law could be hard on battered women who hit back. So, in the early hours I came up with a plan. We buried Frank here." He nodded towards the grass trees. "And I took his place."

She thought of the kind and gentle woman she knew Greta to be. She should have been horrified by what they'd done in covering a crime, but Amy felt only anger towards the man that had abused Greta and sadness for what Frank and Greta must have gone through.

"But didn't anyone realise you weren't Frank?" she asked. "Friends? Family? Someone must have known."

Frank shook his head. "They'd been in Queensland for thirty-five years. Everyone they knew was either dead or had moved on. Besides, Frank had become a recluse, refusing to leave the house." He chuckled. "I shaved my head to look more like that baldy old bastard. Greta and I kept to ourselves. No one knew until four years ago when Ron Foxhall, Frank's brother, got out of prison and came home. Speaking of complicated. Ron. Another damn bloodsucker. The money was to be for Greta's care, for private nurses so she could stay at home when her condition deteriorated." He looked at Amy, his gaze unwavering. "I didn't take any pleasure in killing Ron, but I don't regret it either."

His deep blue eyes searched her face. She wasn't sure what he expected to see. Judgement? Condemnation? After everything she'd heard, Amy felt neither and only pity for the Greta and the Frank that she knew.

Ron Foxhall, the man who was murdered. It all made sense. Amy thought of the instances when Greta was confused and referred to Frank as though he was in her past. And that final morning she'd kept asking for Jim.

"So, Ron was blackmailing you," Amy speculated. "And I'm guessing your real name is Jim?"

"Ron was bleeding us dry, so I killed him." He spoke the words dispassionately. "And you're right. I'm Jim Cole." He rolled his shoulders. "Now you know everything."

He stood, unfolding himself slowly and pressing a hand to a spot just above his stomach. Standing over her, he cast a shadow that blocked out the sunlight.

"Now what?" Amy asked, not sure if she was ready for the answer.

"Now," Frank began, "I need a second cup of coffee and a comfortable chair while I work out the kinks in my back." As he spoke, he was already on the move.

Amy scrambled to her feet and called after him. "But aren't you worried I'll go to the police?"

He stopped and turned back. "I don't care anymore. Just give me a few days to say goodbye to Greta. That's all I ask."

By the time they reached the house, Amy's hair was a sweaty tangle and her clothes were damp with perspiration. While Frank made coffee she went upstairs and did what she could to make herself feel human again.

When she returned, Amy paused in the kitchen doorway. Frank was pulling bread out of the toaster and slathering it with butter.

"I won't," she said. "I mean I won't go to the police."

"Okay," he said and the ghost of what was once a dazzling smile crossed his face. "Now eat."

Neither of them wanted to remain in the kitchen so they sat on the back deck. Amy didn't think she could stomach food, but surprised herself by devouring two slices of toast. With her belly full, she felt strong enough to face the problem at hand.

"I tried to tell you last night," she began. "About Zane and Spider. They think you're a loose end. I told them you had more money." She pushed on trying to explain. "I only did it to stall them while I came to warn you. I don't know what they're planning, but it's not safe for you here."

If Frank was alarmed, he gave no indication. Drinking his coffee, he appeared unfazed.

"They're dangerous," Amy tried again. "Last night I didn't tell you everything."

She'd been dreading this moment, knowing what she had to say would cause him more anguish. He'd been through so much she almost considered keeping the truth from him, but it was lies and cover-ups that had brought her to this point. She didn't think she could carry any more weight on her already over-burdened conscience. Besides, didn't Frank have the right to know the truth?

"Greta didn't fall." She'd blurted out the words. "Zane pushed her."

Frank set down his cup, his movements slow and precise. A look crossed his face, dark and hard, an expression that sent a chill down her spine.

"Frank, please don't–" A knock on the front door, thunderously loud, cut off what she was about to say.

"Stay here," he said, already out of his chair and heading inside the house.

Chapter Twenty-six

With his mind still reeling from what Amy had revealed, Frank opened the door. There was rage bubbling inside him and seeing Worsten standing on his doorstep only fuelled his emotions. It was the detective's fault Greta was dead. Worsten had kept him at the station while Amy's weasel of a boyfriend was killing the only woman he'd ever loved.

"What do you want?" He didn't bother to cover his anger.

The detective's eyes widened with surprise. "I know this probably isn't a good time for you, but I wanted you to hear this from me before you saw it on the news."

"What?" Frank asked confused by what the cop was saying.

"Look, just give me a few minutes," Worsten said and moved to step forward.

Frank stepped out onto the veranda and pulled the door half-closed behind him. "Whatever you have to say, do it here."

The detective seemed ready to protest, but instead simply nodded. "Okay, I'll make this quick."

Frank got the feeling the cop was waiting for him to respond, but he had no idea what Worsten was talking about.

"Your brother's murder. We have the man responsible in custody," the detective continued. "We haven't released his name, but the arrest will be on the news tonight. I wanted to tell you myself." He paused. "Are you okay? You look pale."

"I'm okay." Frank's response was automatic. "Who is he, the man you've arrested?"

"I can't discuss the details, not yet. But at least it's over. It's one less thing for you to deal with."

Frank moved his head, trying to nod and look relieved. At the same time an avalanche of questions was running through his mind.

"I know it's a lot to take in," Worsten said. "If you want, I can arrange for a Victim Liaison Officer to contact you. It might help you sort through everything that's happened."

"No." The word came out with too much force. "Thanks, but that's not necessary."

A few moments ago Frank was angry at the world. He was looking for someone to aim that fury at, but now he realised Worsten wasn't responsible for Greta's death. Worsten was only a man trying to do his job and was showing Frank more kindness than he deserved.

"Is there someone you can call to come and stay with you?" Worsten continued. "A friend or your neighbour? It's not good to be alone at a time like this."

"Yes," Frank said, grappling for the correct response. "You're right. I think I will see my neighbour."

"Good. You do that," Worsten said. He seemed ready to leave, but hesitated. "I really am sorry about your wife."

Moments later when Frank closed the door, he felt like he'd fallen into a nightmare, some kind of bad dream where he was stumbling from one disaster to the next.

Someone had been arrested for a murder he had committed. An innocent man sat in custody, probably facing a lifetime in prison. Frank couldn't let that happen. And then there was Amy's boyfriend, the man who'd come into their home and murdered Greta. Frank leaned against the door and covered his face with his hands. There were wrongs he needed to put right.

Amy was waiting for him in the kitchen. He was struck by how pale and haunted she looked. With the realisation came another pang of guilt. She was a victim in all this as surely as Greta and the man in custody for a crime he hadn't committed.

"Was that the police?" Amy asked. "What did they want?"

Frank leaned against the island. He relayed the information Worsten had given and watched Amy's expression turn from fear to panic.

"What should we do?" she asked, rubbing at her temple.

"There is no we," Frank corrected. "I want you as far away from this as possible. You need to pack a bag and drive back to Perth tonight."

Amy held her hands up in surprise. "And do what? Zane and Spider know where I live. The police will find me wherever I go. Besides, I'm not leaving you alone, not when I'm the reason you're in this mess."

As frustrated as he was with her stubbornness, he was also struck by the change in her. Less than two months ago Amy was incapable of voicing an opinion or starting a sentence without an apology. She'd changed or maybe circumstances had altered her. Either way she was stronger, more confident. But as much as it pained him, now wasn't the time for personal growth.

"Okay," Frank tried again. "But you can't go back to that house."

Amy started to protest, but he pushed on, knowing what she was about to say.

"You can't stay here either. It's not safe. There's a motel in town. I'll pay for your room," he continued, ignoring the wounded look on her face. "That way you'll be nearby, but they won't know where you are."

She was listening now so he pushed on. "Leave your boyfriend a note." He snapped his fingers in thought. "Tell him you're leaving. That you don't want to be involved."

Amy nodded. "What about you?" she asked. "You could come with me."

He hated lying to her, but it was the only way. He needed to know she was safely out of the way, at least for the next few days.

"I will, but give me a few days. I have to make the funeral arrangements. After that I'll get some money together and we'll disappear for a while. My guess is Zane and Spider won't hang around long. Once this blows over, we'll sort out what to do next."

He was telling her what she needed to hear, but there was a small part of him that wished it was true. That there could be some future where he was at peace and able to live out his last days with someone he cared about. Not for the first time, he thought of the daughter that he and Greta had made together and how different life could have been.

"What about the money?" she asked. "I know where it's hidden, I could get it for you."

"Leave it." Frank had plans for the money, but for now she didn't need to know any more. "If you take the money, they'll never let you go."

Amy looked unconvinced, but agreed. "I need to get my things. My clothes and phone charger."

Chapter Twenty-seven

"Okay," Frank said. "The car's gone."

They were on the front veranda. For the last two hours Frank had been making regular checks on the black Holden. At two o'clock it finally pulled out of the driveway.

"Get in and out as quickly as possible. If either one of them is still in the house, back out pronto." Frank looked worried.

"I've already packed," Amy said, heading down the path. "It'll only take a few minutes to grab my suitcase and charger."

"Call me when you get to the motel." Frank's voice followed her as she made her way to the street.

Just as Frank had said, Spider's car was gone. Now all she had to do was grab her things and drive away. A simple task yet the thought of entering the house made her stomach contract.

Inside, the place sat quiet. No trace of either man. Still, Amy didn't waste any time. She went straight to the bedroom and grabbed her suitcase, lugging it into the lounge room.

She'd lived at number five Cobblestone Lane for well over a month, but now she felt like a trespasser, like a stranger on enemy ground. With the curtains still drawn, the house was gloomy with shadows.

Trying to recall just where she'd left the charger, she went through to the kitchen. After only twenty-four hours, the sink was piled with dirty dishes, the bin was overflowing, and a furious buzz of flies filled the air.

It was like seeing the house through fresh eyes or eyes that were finally open. A shabby building, depressing and old, now dirty and permeated with unpleasant smells. This was never a home. She could see that now.

The charger was usually on the counter next to the electric kettle, but save a sticky spill of coffee granules this area sat clear. A quick search of the drawers and cupboards turned up nothing.

"Damn." Amy stood in the centre of the room and ran a hand over her eyes. *Think*.

She was struggling to remember the last time she charged her phone, let alone where. Painfully aware of each passing minute, she moved through the house. Not caring about the mess, she tossed sofa cushions aside and threw open cupboards. At the same time she listened for sounds of a car pulling into the driveway.

The safest option would be to give up and get the hell out, but without the charger she'd be cut off from the world. That's when she thought of the bathroom.

Sure enough, the charger was still plugged into the socket near the sink. Her relief was overwhelming; it brought tears to her eyes. When did she become such a tragic mess? Feeding off the emotions that had surfaced, she snatched the charger and shoved it in her pocket.

Back in the kitchen, she remembered Frank's instructions about leaving a note. There was something else she had to do, but couldn't quite capture the thought. Rather than waste time worrying, she pulled a McDonald's bag out of the bin and tossed it on the table. She used her forearm to iron out the creases.

"Pen?" She spoke to the empty room then remembered seeing a pen in one of the kitchen drawers. Hands shaking, she yanked out the drawer with too much force. Cutlery clattered to the floor.

Watching knives, forks, and spoons scatter and bounce, she felt a surge of wildness. Amy threw the drawer across the room. It hit the fridge and landed with a satisfying crack.

A burst of laughter bubbled up her throat and broke free. She clamped her hand over her mouth, but couldn't supress the giggles. Was this what madness felt like? Crying in the bathroom and hysterical laughter in the kitchen? Was the insanity coming from her or oozing out of the timbre of the hateful house?

Still on a manic high, she scrambled around on the floor until she found the pen. When she scrawled the note, it was as if a kind of craziness had taken her over.

> *I never want to see you again. Enjoy the money, you murdering bastard.*

Amy barked out a laugh, not realising how hard she was squeezing the pen until it snapped in her hand. Ink covered her fingers like blue blood. Without thinking, she wiped her hands on the paper bag, leaving inky prints around the words she'd written. Not satisfied with the mess, she wiped the remaining ink on the table and then the fridge.

She was busy running her fingers over the cupboards when the madness of what she was doing hit her. The destructive outburst ended as suddenly as it began leaving her breathless and exhausted.

Panicked by what she'd done, Amy rinsed her hands under the tap. Earlier she'd been afraid to enter the house and now she was horrified by her own actions. Not wanting to look at the mayhem any longer, she ran through the house only pausing long enough to grab her suitcase.

* * *

The motel room was basic, but clean and comfortable. Her phone was dead so she set it to charge while she showered and put on clean clothes.

Being away from Cobblestone Lane did more to sooth her nerves than all the shampooing and washing could achieve. It didn't matter that she could hear the hum of traffic or bursts of conversation from the parking lot. In the characterless room she felt a sense of normality returning, a feeling she wanted to soak up if only for a few hours.

As much as she was worried about Frank and how he was alone next door to Zane and Spider, she craved the sense of peace the distance afforded. With the phone functioning, she opted to text Frank rather than make a call.

She let him know she was safe then sat on the bed combing her damp hair and watching afternoon TV. With the television volume turned up, she could almost shut out the voice in her head that told her that by trashing the house she'd made things worse for herself *and* Frank.

Chapter Twenty-eight

Frank watched Amy drive away then went back inside. Twenty minutes later he put what he needed in the car and pulled out of the driveway. As he passed the neighbour's house he noted that there was still no sign of the black Holden.

They'd be back, the two men responsible for Greta's death. He was sure of it. He clung to that belief because he had plans for them. He'd be ready, but for now Frank had arrangements to make.

Maybe it was sheer force of will, but whatever the reason the pain had abated. He knew better than to believe the reprieve was permanent. It would be back, possibly worse than before. For now he'd take the respite and make the most of it. What other choice did he have?

His first stop was the funeral home; an unremarkable building. If not for the tasteful sign in muted burgundy hues, the place could have been mistaken for a squat, industrial office.

Frank parked near the entrance and killed the engine. He allowed himself a moment to gather his strength. Hands draped over the steering wheel, he tried to imagine

Greta as she once was, but all he could summon was the memory of her last moments.

Who are you? What are you doing here?

Those words hadn't been a glitch in her brain, but a frantic message. She'd been trying to tell him what happened, a dying effort to communicate what had been done to her. Frank clamped his hands to the side of his head trying to push out the images that filled his mind – images his imagination had conjured up to torture him. Greta trying to run. That filthy animal putting his hands on her. For that more than anything else he hated the men responsible.

He should have had time to grieve. Greta deserved that much, but that too had been taken away from him. Now all he had was his anger and a few minutes to deliver her clothes and say goodbye.

"I'm sorry, my darling," he said, staring at the building that now housed the woman he loved. "There should have been more than this." Not giving himself the opportunity to crumple, he stepped out of the car.

After the undertaker, he checked his phone and found a message from Amy letting him know she was safely ensconced at the motel. Apart from losing Greta, dragging Amy into this mess was his biggest regret. If things went the way he planned, he'd never see the girl again. That realisation tugged at his heart with surprising strength. After years of isolating themselves, it was strange they'd both become so fond of Amy. Or perhaps she represented something they'd lost.

He'd opened the parcel after Amy left. The last thing Greta had ordered turned out to be a leather music book embossed with Amy's name. Inside the book was a collection of sheet music, pages Greta wanted Amy to learn. Sharing her gift for music with Amy had made Greta happy. Not just happy, but energised. Now the book and the music were a reminder of what was lost for both women.

Turning his thoughts back to the matter at hand, Frank drove on. This next stop would be his last. As the streets flew by, he had a sense that the world was narrowing and everything around him, the people, cars and mundane concerns were falling away. It was a feeling of lightness that wasn't altogether unpleasant. There was no fear, just a growing acceptance of the inevitable.

It would be finished soon, tonight most likely or tomorrow at the latest. With acceptance came calm. He parked and entered his solicitor's office determined to do some good before he left every shred of his humanity behind. It was the best he could do.

* * *

Frank found what he needed in the garage. It took fifty minutes to put his plan together then he made two trips into the house, setting items in place. Planning and double checking was second nature to him and the process was made easier because this time he wouldn't need an alibi. This time there was no need to cover his tracks.

They would come; he was sure of it. They'd wait for the cover of darkness and that worked for him too. Long ago in the jungles of Vietnam he'd discovered it was easier to kill with only the moon as a witness.

What he'd done to Ron sickened him, but it had been necessary to protect what he had with Greta. Tonight was different. There were no scruples clouding his resolve *and* no consequences, only justice for Greta. For that he'd give his soul, what was left of it.

As evening drew in, Frank took up his position on the veranda. When darkness fell, he heard the Holden approaching so he walked the path to the street as an open invitation he hoped they'd accept.

The car slowed but didn't stop. It coasted past Frank and then turned in a lazy arc. With the outside light on, Frank knew the men could see him watching their progress.

Youth and arrogance would entice them. Frank counted on it as he continued his surveillance and saw them turn into next door's driveway. Satisfied they'd taken the bait, he went back inside.

As he moved through the house, every creak and tick was as familiar as his own body: sounds that mapped the landscape of the old house. He'd hear them before they appeared.

In the kitchen he used a chair to climb up and loosen the light bulb then he repeated the process in the hall. Next, Frank turned on the side lamp in the sitting room and set up what he needed on the far side of his armchair. He sat and reached down, practising the motion until the movement was swift and fluid.

Working with greater speed now, he placed a backup weapon behind the kitchen door. Be prepared, he thought without a trace of mirth. Finally, he moved halfway up the stairs where he crouched and made more adjustments. Standing, he tested what he created and was satisfied it would do the job.

Descending the last few steps, he reached for the railing, but drew back. A tingling sensation ran over his hand and up his forearm. Frank flexed his fingers then made a fist while he cursed under his breath. To get through tonight he needed to be quick with his hands. A second later, the tingling passed and he was able to continue with his preparations.

When everything was ready, he unlocked the back and front doors then returned to the sitting room. He poured himself a splash of whiskey, enough to settle his nerves but not so much it would dull his reflexes. Before sitting, he put on a record with the volume turned low.

Now he would wait. He would wait as long as it took. Zane and Spider were forty years younger than him. Spider. He had no doubt the punk had given himself that name because he thought it made him sound tough. From what Frank had seen of them, the two men looked pretty soft. They were adept at pushing women around, but what about a grown man? Frank's body was failing, he knew that, but his reactions were still sharp. He had a size advantage and the element of surprise on his side. But would it be enough?

Chapter Twenty-nine

"She said he didn't know," Spider said killing the engine. "Did you see him? He was watching us. Do you think she told him?"

"He knows," Zane said climbing out of the car. He nodded to the space Amy's car usually occupied. "She's gone." He'd spoken over his shoulder as he stomped off towards the house.

Spider followed. He didn't like the bitterness in Zane's voice. Who cared if she was gone? Having her around had been a pain in the ass. All he cared about was getting the money and getting the hell out of Bunbury.

"Jesus." Zane stopped short in the doorway.

Looking over his shoulder at the trashed lounge room, Spider's first thought was a break-in and almost instantly his mind went to the money. Leaving Zane still staring at the destruction in the sitting room, Spider sprinted through the house and into the laundry.

When he reached the dryer, he stopped. He couldn't say how he knew but his gut told him the appliance had been moved.

"No. No, no," he muttered, pulling the machine away from the wall.

When he saw the screws were in place, he let out a breath through clenched teeth. He could hear Zane cursing in the kitchen, but the sound was white noise. All that mattered was the money. His money.

Not wasting time with the screws, he dug his fingers in the gap and tore off the backboard. It was there. The bag was where they'd left it. He was shaking when he dragged the carry-all out and opened the zip. Rolls of cash. He slumped onto the floor and tipped his head back. Everything was okay. The money was safe.

He found Zane in the kitchen holding a paper bag. There were trickles of sweat glistening on his temple and his eyes were glassy.

"Look." Zane tossed the MacDonald's bag on the table.

Spider stepped around the wreckage that covered the floor and picked up the bag. He whistled. "Looks like Splat has some backbone after all."

Spider was laughing at his own observation when Zane rushed him. The attack was so sudden it caught him off guard. Zane's shoulder thumped into Spider's chest and drove him into the wall.

"You think this is funny?" Zane asked, his eyes bulging as warm spittle sprayed Spider's face.

Rather than resist the assault, Spider grabbed Zane's face between his hands and pulled him closer, so close their mouths were only centimetres apart.

"I think you need to get a grip," Spider said in a low voice. "She wasn't part of the plan." He held Zane's gaze. "Or am I missing something?"

"No. I'm just surprised is all," Zane said, his eyes blinking rapidly.

Spider tried to laugh it off, but there was hurt in Zane's voice. If he didn't know better, he'd think Zane was trying not to cry. Yet there had been countless times when Zane swore she was nothing more than a meal ticket – a sweet distraction – but Spider now thought differently.

He'd seen the way Zane touched her, the way he defended her. What Spider couldn't understand was why she meant so much to him. While Spider was repulsed by her, by anything freakish, he could see that without the birthmark she could be pretty: a wholesome kind of prettiness that together with her eagerness to please might be attractive if you liked that sort of thing.

Could Zane really want that? The Zane he knew was turned on by danger and was attracted to darkness. Yet there was a part of Spider that wondered if Zane was attracted to the life Amy represented. Was it the promise of that wholesome lifestyle more than Amy herself that had seduced him?

The anger went out of Zane's face and he leaned into Spider, their foreheads touching.

"We don't need her," Spider whispered. "You never needed her. Not like this." He cupped his hands around the back of Zane's neck. "We have the money. We can do whatever we want."

He could feel Zane's heart beating against his through the thin fabric of his T-shirt. There was urgency in the way Zane grabbed Spider's shoulders, but also violence. This was what Spider craved. Zane's desperate need was more important than money or sex. To be craved beyond anything else made Spider *feel*. It cut through the numbness as surely as a blade.

His mind went to Travis and what they'd done to the young homeless man, luring him in with the promise of drugs and a warm place to sleep. It was unplanned. Just a bit of fun that became so much more. The unmatched high that came with watching Travis's eyes when he realised what was happening to him. He felt Travis's fear and it was more powerful than anything he'd ever experienced. The memory made Spider shiver.

At fourteen he began cutting himself, small sharp slices on his thigh. When the blade broke through his skin, Spider felt awake. The pain made colours sharper and sounds crisper and the dullness of existence turned into a rush. But the scars were ugly and ugly wasn't his thing.

Spider then found something better than cutting. Through a relationship with an older married man, he discovered power over others. Turning someone inside out because they craved him became thrilling. Making a grown man do whatever he wanted was like a drug.

By the time he was eighteen he'd had a spider tattooed over the scars on his thigh. He changed his appearance, dying his hair and working hard to develop a muscular body lean and toned. Spider moved on to Perth's bars and nightclubs. There he became adept at finding older men all too eager to be used and manipulated. The sense of power was intoxicating. He lived for it until that night with Travis.

Travis, through his death, introduced Spider to a new thrill. Fear. Travis's fear. Spider's *own* fear. Remembering the sensation and the way his heart had beat so hard, he thought he might die. It was a memory he only allowed himself to examine in small doses. Something fragile and precious like a dried flower. With each handling, the pleasure faded.

"Remember Travis," Spider whispered, running his fingers through Zane's hair. "You were so scared, but in the end you liked it."

Zane's breathing eased. He was listening, relaxing. Spider pushed him away and walked around the table, enjoying the feeling of Zane's eyes on him. He leaned his back against the sink and ran a hand over his pale hair.

"The flights are booked. We have money. Let's go visit the old man and find out what he knows."

A slow smile spread over Zane's face. "We can ask him where the rest of the money is hidden."

"Yeah." Spider liked the idea and not just because of the money. "Splat said there was more. We just need to convince him to tell us where it is."

* * *

Spider stepped out onto the back deck where the light was fading and turning the sky into a purple smudge. He rolled a joint which he laced with meth. A few drags would heighten his senses and enhance the night's experience. He'd share it with Zane. The smoke would ease their jitters.

Again, Spider's thoughts turned to Amy. He was happy she'd split, but as night approached and the anticipation grew he wished she'd hung around. He was looking forward to having some fun with the old man, but Splat would have been sweeter – a memory to really savour.

He lit the joint and drew in, holding the smoke in his lungs. What, he wondered, would it feel like to make Zane watch while he played with Amy? The idea together with the meth sent a charge of excitement that surged through his body like an electric current.

A moment later, Spider found Zane in the lounge room. He could see by the pout that he was still brooding over her.

Spider held out the joint. "Here," he said. "Time to make some magic."

Zane wanted to refuse. Spider could see it in his eyes. He could also see Zane's desperate need to please him overtake his misgivings about what they were about to do. Zane took the joint and put it to his lips, reminding Spider of an obedient child. He was nervous and too proud to back out. He sucked on the blunt like it was oxygen and when he plucked it out of his mouth, Zane's hands were shaking.

It occurred to Spider that Zane had become too easy to manipulate. Maybe he was broken. For Spider, broken things were dull. It might be time for Spider to move on. Once they were finished with the old man, he'd have to consider his options.

Chapter Thirty

A text appeared on her phone: her mother asking her to call her back. Amy covered her face with her hands. The last thing she wanted was to answer questions about her life, about her relationship.

While alone in the motel room she'd had plenty of time to ponder her situation. What else was there to do within the four walls? She'd had such high hopes for her life with Zane and now they were shattered. No. Worse than that. Her life was a mess of lies, and murder, and theft, a seedy downslide into something dark and out of control.

The person who'd packed up and moved to Bunbury with childish dreams of a picture-perfect life was only a memory. A pathetic girl that had tried to make a shabby house seem like a home and had dreamed of planting a garden. Now, she was caught up in a nightmare – a nightmare that started with Travis.

Amy picked up her phone. There were four messages, all from her mother. At some point she'd have to tell her what happened. Because it didn't matter how she looked at it, she was guilty. She'd helped Zane cover up the young man's death. She'd kept their secret and never allowed herself to wonder about Travis's family and how dumping his body in a doorway had impacted their lives.

Amy wasn't innocent in all this. Was it any wonder her life had fallen apart? Was it any wonder picture perfect didn't work when you tried to build it on a secret? *Picture perfect.* The thought brought her back to the photos, the images of Ron and Frank: the other Frank. Like the sensation of falling, her stomach flipped. In her rush to pack, she'd left the photos behind.

"Oh no." She leapt off the bed. Her earlier self-pity forgotten, she began to pace.

She remembered putting the photos inside a packet of sanitary pads. She'd then put the packet in the bathroom cabinet. At the time she'd thought it the perfect hiding place, the one place Zane and Spider would be too squeamish to check. Now all she could think of was how stupid she was not only by keeping such incriminating evidence but leaving it behind where either of the two men might discover it.

Her mind went to Detective Worsten. What if he returned with more questions? What if he came back with a search warrant? It was a stretch, but she was helpless to stop the crazy chain of what-ifs.

She was still holding the phone, pacing the six steps between the door and the window when the mobile rang in her hand. Amy's first thought was Zane, but when she looked at the screen she saw it was her mother. Without hesitating, she dismissed the call only to receive a text seconds later.

> *Please tell me what's going on. I'm worried!!! If I don't hear from you, I'm driving there tonight.*

"Damn." She stopped pacing.

Her mother didn't make idle threats. If Amy didn't think fast, she risked having her mother and little sister involved. Amy thought of Spider and the way he'd ground his fist into her ribs and then of watching Zane's hand hit Greta between the shoulders. There was no way she could let her family come anywhere near Bunbury.

She closed her eyes and took a long breath which she held while counting to three. When she had her emotions under control, she called home.

"Amy." Her mother answered on the first ring. "Are you all right? What's going on?"

Catherine Holt was afraid. The most solid person Amy had ever known was shaken. She'd realised that by not answering her calls and texts she was letting her mother worry. In the midst of what was going on, Amy hadn't stopped to really take in how her behaviour would affect her mother. Hearing the panic in her mother's voice made her feel sick with guilt.

"I'm okay, just upset." She didn't have to fake the tremor in her voice. "Zane and I broke up."

"Oh sweetheart, are you okay?" There was relief as well as concern in her mother's voice. A break-up was normal, something distressing but also something that could be gotten over.

"Yes, I will be," Amy continued. "He moved out and I guess I stopped answering my phone for a while. Sorry if I worried you."

"Come home," her mother pleaded.

Come home. Amy screwed up her eyes and clenched her teeth, using all her will to stifle a sob. She wanted to be home so badly it hurt.

"I will." She tried to keep her tone even. "I'm just going take a day or two. You know, pack, clean the house and let work know."

"Do you want me to come?" Catherine asked. "I could help you clean. You don't have to do it all alone."

"Thanks, Mum, but I do." Finally, she was being truthful. "I'm going to sort this out myself. I'll call you tomorrow and let you know when I'll be home."

She hated all the lies, but it was safer than the truth. Safer for her mother anyway. Besides, there was some truth in what she'd said, at least the part about having to sort things out for herself. And the photos were where she'd start.

She should have destroyed them when she had the chance. Now, every minute they were in the house the possibility of Zane or Spider finding them grew. The two men were dangerous: they'd already proved that. Spider had worked out that Frank was hiding something. If they found the pictures, they could use them to blackmail him.

She thought of Frank alone inside that big house. He'd been through so much without this new threat. Amy still worried that the two men would do something to hurt Frank. Not for the first time she wished she'd been able to convince Frank to stay at the motel.

She stood in the middle of the room and tipped her head back. There wasn't much she could do to put things right. All she could fix was the problem of the photos. At least that way she could prevent anyone from finding out what Frank and Greta had done. She could destroy the pictures and protect the two people she'd come to love.

* * *

Amy parked around the corner from Cobblestone Lane. With the headlights turned off, she doubted anyone would notice her car. She remained in the vehicle and pulled Detective Worsten's card out of her pocket. Apart from her keys and phone, it was the only thing she'd brought with her. She turned the card over in her hand.

Calling the detective would put a stop to all the madness and it would guarantee Frank's safety. But how would Frank explain the money? Turning the two men in for killing Greta would make things worse for Frank. He'd be safe, but safely locked away. And, yes, there was part of her that feared her own fate if her part in all this came out. How could she tell the police what really happened without ending up in prison herself? *Prison.* The idea terrified her.

Out of the car and on the dark street, all the possibilities danced around and around in her mind. A puzzle that, no matter how she looked at it, had no solution. Every option brought forth the inevitable: prison for her *and* Frank.

There were a few lights along the lane. As she neared the corner of the world she'd called home for the last few months, the street really did seem like a dark country set apart from a world of life and activity. The sense of menace and foreboding she'd experienced the day they moved in was stronger now, like an almost solid mass of peril.

By the time she neared the house, she had run out of options. The only thing that was clear was her need to retrieve the photos. For this at least she had some kind of plan.

If Spider's car was gone, she'd use her keys and go inside. If the car was still there, she'd go in through the bathroom window. She just prayed the window was still unlocked.

The moon was partially obscured by clouds. In the almost blackness she made out glints of light captured by the Holden's grill. A glow shone out of the lounge room window. They were home.

She slowed her progress, but didn't stop. With the men in the house she'd have to enter through the window. The prospect of being caught inside the house made her weak with fear.

Could she do it? Did she have the courage to even try? If this was a film, she'd be marvelling at the heroine's stupidity, but she realised she was going to go through with the plan. With that knowledge came not calm but a measure of resolve. She crouched low, satisfied she was hidden by shadows and darkness. Zane and Spider viewed her as weak and afraid. They were probably right, but that belief meant they wouldn't expect her to come back. If luck was on her side, maybe she'd get away with what she had in mind.

When she reached the house, she moved closer to the fence where rangy bushes shielded her approach. Stupidity or not, she was going to make up for all the weakness and all the times she should have shown more courage. Now she was going to do the right thing and put someone else first.

Still bent low, she moved along the far side of Spider's car. The plan was to grab the photos and then go next door to Frank. As she hedged closer to the house with the blood rushing in her ears, she became more convinced she was doing the right thing. She'd take the photos to Frank and convince him to come to the motel. She hadn't worked out what she'd say, but there had to be a way. From there, they'd figure out what to do about Zane and Spider.

At the side of the house, she glanced back towards the front yard. The unmistakable shape of the trampoline looked more like a giant creature in the dark. For some reason, she thought of an old movie where a man never ages but his image in a painting grew old and depraved-looking.

Weren't they all guilty of losing themselves to their desires? Money, violence, and love had driven them to unspeakable acts, her included. The aging trampoline might be like that picture and all of the murder and depravity of Cobblestone Lane was reflected in the rusting monstrosity. It was a chilling idea. Ridiculous, but nonetheless unsettling.

Dragging her attention away from the trampoline and back to the house, Amy listened for any noise. When she was satisfied that no one was moving about, she darted towards the house.

Chapter Thirty-one

Spider kept a flick-knife wedged between his skin and the leather of his right boot. He'd used it to threaten, but had never actually stuck anyone with it. He recalled the sound the spring mechanism made when it popped open in front of Travis's face. A click followed by a metallic whoosh. A menacing noise that startled Travis out of his hazy stupor. The sight of the twelve centimetre blade had made Travis's eyes bulge with fear.

Tonight, Spider kept the knife in his hand as they made the silent trip next door. The latex gloves he wore were necessary, but they dulled the feeling of the blade's handle. He'd have preferred skin on metal contact. Behind him, Zane's footfalls were tentative and muffled.

Things were building: the sense of excitement and anticipation. The sensation, not unlike sex, grew with each rhythmic beat of his heart. Spider wished he could prolong the feeling, take his time tapping on the old guy's windows and rattling the doors. He'd like to really get the party going and watch their neighbour sweat.

He glanced over his shoulder to the dark silhouette behind him. With Zane along for the ride, Spider's freedom was to some extent curtailed. *Next time*. Tonight would have to serve as a learning experience. Not a bad thing, he told himself. Yet, his mind longed to explore the possibilities and resented the restraint he would have to show.

They were in the Foxhalls' front yard. The house was dark with no signs of life shining through its windows. Instead of going to the door, they stayed on the grass and walked toward the side gate.

There must have been a light on around the back because Spider could see well enough to spot a chunk of brick keeping the gate open. Maybe Amy wasn't lying about the old man being clueless or perhaps no one had warned their neighbour that an open gate invited visitors.

"Here we go," he said over his shoulder and stepped into the backyard.

Just as he'd guessed, a single light burned on the deck. As unseen insects sang, sweat broke out on Spider's skin. He stopped and looked up at the moon. Every sound, every sensation seemed exquisitely sharp. This night would be one to remember and he intended to savour every minute.

"Come on. What are you waiting for?" Zane asked over Spider's shoulder. "Let's just get this done."

There was an irritating whine to Zane's voice that Spider had never heard before, a voice that shattered the moment and reminded Spider of the limitations of having a partner. Not only was Zane too squeamish, as it turned out his criminal record made it impossible for him to travel to the United States of America.

The best the two men had been able to do was tickets to Thailand. Asia would be a good place to celebrate and then part ways. He'd give it a few days and then take the money and fly to America. Arizona first and then New York City. A lifetime of watching American TV had made it easy for Spider to work on his accent. In fact, accents were something that came easy to him. Not at first. As a kid he saw a film about a man that beat his stutter by developing a completely different accent. In the movie, the guy did it by using accents and staring at his reflection while speaking. It took Spider almost a year and a range of drawls, but eventually he shed the stutter like an ugly skin.

Without his Australian inflection, he'd be able to disappear into the United States. He could move from state to state picking up and dropping twangs. That sort of freedom would open up a world of possibilities.

He didn't bother with the stairs, just jumped onto his haunches on the side of the deck and then span around and sprung to his feet. He was charged, feeling strong. The old man was probably senile, but he *was* big. If things went sideways, it might take the two of them to force the old guy to co-operate so Zane might be useful after all.

Spider stood looking down at Zane. In the light he could see Zane's features. His sexy lips were pressed together making him look like he was about to cry. Spider smiled at him and jerked his head towards the back door.

He was prepared to smash the glass panel and reach through to slide the bolt, but to his relief the door was unlocked. The old guy really was making it too easy. Spider almost felt sorry for him.

As soon as the door opened, he heard the music: a soft old-fashioned tune drifting out from somewhere on the ground floor. So Frank wasn't tucked up in bed? What a shame. Spider had imagined the look in the old guy's eyes when he woke to see them standing over him. But coming up on him while he was awake would do.

Chapter Thirty-two

Despite the heat hanging in the air like limp sheets, Amy felt chilled. Looking at the bathroom window sitting higher up than she remembered, the cold sank beneath her skin to a deeper place. Bone deep.

Jumping and pulling herself up to the window ledge would be noisy; knees thumping and feet scraping in the stillness would attract attention. She needed something to stand on. Thinking of that long-ago day when she'd clambered in through the bathroom, she remembered finding a hunk of concrete pipe sticking out of the weeds like a wonky tooth.

With no other option, she used the light on her phone. Taking care to keep the beam pointed down so as to avoid being seen, she ran the light over the ground. Almost instantly, the light found what she was looking for. A moment later she had the chunk of concrete under the window.

When she stepped up on her makeshift step, it hit her. She was really doing this. She was breaking into her own house under the cover of night. Being caught by Spider would be a grave mistake. *Grave.* The word made her tremble.

When she shoved the partially open window up, what she was doing was entering enemy territory. Territory disguised as harmless, albeit a run-down house. If discovered, the cracked rib and bruised shoulder would be nothing compared to what might happen.

I won't get caught. This thought and a sudden surge of confidence caught her off guard. She'd come a long way, but the urge to back out was still flittering around her mind. If she hesitated, that urge would grow legs and carry her away. Best to keep moving, she thought.

She braced herself, palms flat on the window ledge, then pulled herself up and in before she could talk herself down. Down off the ledge, literally – the thought made her want to giggle. No, not giggle, shriek.

In seconds she was inside, sitting on the sill and sliding down to the bathroom floor. Like a cat burglar, she landed in a crouch only to wince at the echo from her joggers hitting the tiles. Frozen to the spot, she waited for the sound of voices or running feet. Any indications she'd been heard and Amy intended to hot foot it back the way she came.

For an instant, there was the sound of thundering footfalls, but she quickly realised what she heard was her own blood drubbing in her ears.

"It's okay." She wasn't sure if she'd whispered the words or just thought them. As long as no one heard, she didn't much care.

She was in! There was a second of elation before she remembered getting in was the easy part. Now she had to locate the photos and get the hell out without getting caught.

Turning the light on was out of the question so again she used her phone. The instant the blue light appeared, Amy spotted a figure crouched in the darkness and gasped. The phone slipped out of her right hand, but miraculously she caught it with her left at the same time she realised the figure was her reflection in the mirror over the sink.

If her heart was pounding before, now it was booming. If she didn't calm down, she risked losing her balance and falling or having a full-blown panic attack. Resisting the desire to rush, she lowered herself to the floor and sat. She put her head between her knees. Wasn't that what you were supposed to do? Five breaths, she told herself. Take five and then stand.

It felt like an eternity, but she stayed the course. After expelling the fifth lung-full, she stood. Her heart wasn't exactly resting, but had slowed.

"All right then." This time she did most definitely speak the words, a whisper, but a steady one.

She moved with care, opening the cabinet and directing the beam. The packet was where she'd left it, right behind a three-pack of Dove soap. Luckily, Zane and Spider were happy to walk around encased in their own filth or they might have reached for the soap and noticed the unusual bulge in the packet of sanitary pads.

She pulled the packet from its place and shook out the photographs. A quick count proved all three pictures were there. Satisfied, she stuck the photos down the back of her jeans and returned the packet to its original spot. Before closing the cupboard, she adjusted the soap so that it appeared nothing had been touched. Not that the two men would notice, but it didn't hurt to be careful. *Careful was what I should have been on the day I met Zane.*

Glancing down, she noticed the time: just past nine o'clock. Something about that seemed odd. Under the circumstances, breaking into her own house to recover evidence of a murder, it was unclear just what that something was.

Instead of exiting, she stayed crouched in front of the cabinet. In the unbroken silence it dawned on her that the lack of noise was the anomaly. No TV, no voices, no music, and no movement.

She turned off the light on her phone and cracked the door a few centimetres. There was light in the hall, filtering through from the lounge, but no sound save the steady drip from the kitchen tap. Was it a trick?

She had what she'd come for. The rational thing to do would be to leave the way she'd come in. But could she go without being sure? With Spider's car in the driveway and the two men gone, it could mean only one thing. They'd gone somewhere on foot. Her mind made the only leap that seemed logical: Frank. Yes, that had to be it, but she had to be sure.

She edged her way along the hall. With each step she became more convinced that the house was empty. A quick glance into the lounge revealed the light had been left on and the room sat unoccupied. The kitchen was also empty. Checking the bedrooms was somewhat more daunting. In for a penny, she told herself even though she'd never really understood that expression. She opened the door to the main bedroom, the one she'd shared with Zane back in the days before she'd watched him murder Greta.

Still too afraid to turn on the lights, she shone her phone light around the room. For a blink, she imagined Spider with his arms folded over his bare chest like a tattooed vampire. Another blink and the room was empty. Just an unmade bed and a bunch of drawers hanging open. All the signs of her rapid exit.

The spare room was a different story. A more terrifying prospect because part of her was more afraid of what she might see when she shone her light into the darkness than what the two men would do to her if she stumbled upon them.

In the end, the room revealed nothing more frightening than dirty unmade sheets, piles of soiled clothing and a collection of empty beer bottles. As she grimaced at the thick stench of sweat and stale beer, it occurred to her that she'd been insane to live with these people. Not wanting to explore the thought any more than she wanted to breathe the tainted air, she pulled the door closed.

She went back to the kitchen and called Frank. It was possible that Zane and Spider were just out for the evening doing God knows what. Partying? Selling drugs? Hurting someone? Still, she ought to give Frank the heads up. Aside from all that, she wanted to hear his voice; that calm tone that made things seem clearer; the perfect mixture of stony and gentle.

The call went straight to messages where Frank's gravelly if somewhat stilted voice told her to leave a message and a phone number. The message was so typical of him, no window dressing, just straight to business.

She hesitated, not sure what to say or how much to commit to the recording. "It's Amy, um. I don't know where they are. Be careful."

She hung up hoping the message wasn't too cryptic and if Frank was already asleep it wouldn't matter. As she put her phone away, she noticed two things: a yellow disposable lighter and Zane's phone. Both were on the counter.

There was one way to make sure no one ever discovered Frank's secret. She took the lighter and grabbed the photos out of her jeans. She stood at the sink and flicked it, then taking them one by one she touched the flame to each picture.

In a matter of minutes, all three curled and turned black before she dropped them into the sink where they disintegrated. Finally, she set the third picture alight. The wedding photo blackened as Greta's young face was consumed by fire. Losing her again was like a fresh wound.

When she finished it occurred to her that destroying evidence was just the latest in her growing list of crimes. She thought of the *in for a penny* saying again and now it made more sense, then used the edge of her T-shirt to wipe the lighter clean of her prints.

With the photos gone, she planned to leave, but Zane's phone was calling to her. She had no real objective in mind when she picked up the mobile, just a vague idea that it might give her some insight into what the two men were up to. It also puzzled her that he'd go anywhere and leave it behind. Not that he was glued to it, but still.

Now that she had it in her hand with no danger of Zane catching her, she thought she might as well take a peek. At the same time there was a voice inside her whispering that she'd never be able to unsee whatever secrets the mobile held. The same voice that used to tell her Zane was using her. Then, like now, she had ignored that sensible voice.

His password was easy: 4321. Not very clever as passwords go, but Amy was beginning to realise Zane wasn't that bright. He was a good liar and an even better actor, but not smart. She'd fallen for every word that came out of his mouth so she supposed that made her pretty dumb too. Was trust a stupid thing?

She tapped the password into the keypad and watched the screen open. *I'm wising up now.* A little late but better late than never. That one made more sense than the penny saying. Too late to help Greta but maybe there was still time to stop things getting worse.

She started with texts, scrolling through the ones from Spider. Nothing jumped out, not a first.

> *Zane: That thing will have to wait. She's always home.*
> *Spider: No rush. Wait for Splat to go to work.*

Splat. Amy stared at the nickname scarcely able to believe her eyes. She'd really believed Zane couldn't hurt her any more than he already had. Boy was she wrong, so wrong it was almost funny. He'd told Spider about the humiliating name; worse than that, they'd made it their personal inside joke.

While she was working at Day Mart, buying groceries, cooking meals and worrying about rent, Spider and Zane had been laughing at her. Instead of tears, something hard was building in her chest. Had Zane told Spider about her pathetic attempts in the bedroom? How she'd beg him to touch her or the shameful ways she had tried to please him?

The phone was shaking in her hand and tears *were* coming now. Hot angry tears that stung her eyes. She wanted to smash the phone against the wall. Her mind searched for some way to hurt them the way they'd hurt her. But most of all, she wished she could dig her nails into the disgusting birthmark and claw it off her face.

In the end, she did none of those things. Instead, she went to the laundry and dragged the carry-all out of its hiding place. She pulled out a roll of cash and took it back to the kitchen and tossed it on the draining board. This was what the two men cared about.

With Zane's phone in one hand and the lighter in the other, she was careful to keep herself out of the footage. She filmed the wad of money going up in flames. Well, smoke mostly because of the plastic, but it was still pretty cool. When she finished, she sent the footage to Spider with a one word message: *Splat.*

Once the film was delivered, she sat at the table and cradled her head in her hands. The satisfaction of only a moment ago had ebbed into something that was closer to dismay. There was no regret, just a feeling of numbness. What had she achieved outside of putting a target on her back?

With the camera function still open and the phone sitting between her elbows, she noticed an image in the bottom left corner of the screen. When she tapped it, a picture of Spider leaning on the roof of his Holden filled the screen, a lock of his bleached hair falling over his pale eyes as he stared into the camera not quite smiling. Amy tutted at the image and continued to scroll through the album.

One image after another all of the same man, some posed like the first one with the car, others candid shots of

Spider walking an unfamiliar street or drinking from a beer bottle. Another of him sitting on the back deck smoking a joint. She whistled out a breath. So many photographs of the same subject, images taken by an adoring eye. Images that told a story of obsession that went far beyond anything she'd ever suspected.

She'd lived with Zane and had shared a bed with him. So many days and nights believing they were in love when in truth she knew nothing about him. Had none of it been real? What purpose had she served in Zane's life? Seeing the photos her boyfriend had taken left her astounded by the depths of her own blindness and naivety.

If only she'd gone through his phone months ago so much hurt and damage could have been avoided. But would she have taken in what was so clear? Or would she have formulated excuses like she'd done countless times over the last year? Wearing blinkers allowed her to willingly live in a fool's paradise. She could at least see *that* now.

It should have been enough. The photos of Spider should have hurt her sufficiently that she left the phone alone, but she couldn't do that. Now that her eyes were open, she wanted every painful truth. That's when she came upon Travis.

The picture caught her eye because it was the only one that wasn't of Spider. She'd never seen Travis in anything but an unconscious state, yet he was immediately recognisable, his face still and youthful despite the sunken cheeks and pallor.

Because the image was a close-up, it almost filled the screen. What was also clearly evident was the crescent-shaped cut beneath his eye, a fresh wound still raw and angry-looking. There was a bare arm around his shoulders. The limb's owner was out of sight, but his tattoos were clearly visible. Amy didn't need to see the face to recognise those tattoos and know the arm belonged to Spider.

Judging by the cut on Travis's face, the picture was taken not long before he died. The photo also proved that Zane wasn't the only person with Travis in the time leading up to his death. Both men were with Travis before he overdosed.

Her mind was grappling with this new information and what it might mean. Still gazing at the photo, something else became clear. At first glance Travis appeared to be smiling, but the longer she stared at his expression the more it looked like the grin was pained or not a grin at all but a grimace.

Amy didn't think it was a grimace or a grin. She thought Travis looked scared – a scared kid told to smile for the camera, a smile that brought fresh tears to her eyes. And Spider's arm wasn't around Travis, but clutching him.

The longer she looked at the photograph the more certain Amy was that she was seeing something dark and perverse. Zane's phone was a tome of secrets and horrors. Just holding the thing made her feel unclean. At the same time she couldn't let Travis's image go because doing so would be like abandoning him a second time.

She pulled out her phone and photographed the image. Her hands were still tied when it came to what happened to Greta. She'd played a part in Travis's death just as she had in Greta's. Maybe she could put things right for one of them.

Chapter Thirty-three

The kitchen was in darkness save the light creeping in from the deck. The illumination fell on the marble chopping block in yellow bands. A soft *plink* from behind told Spider that Zane had entered the kitchen and had closed the door.

Being back in this room reminded him of the old woman. Zane hadn't hesitated, probably because he pushed her from behind. Not having to look her in the eyes would have made it easier for him. Sort of cowardly in Spider's opinion, but it had gotten the job done.

The music was still playing, some ancient French song that drifted through the house. Spider grabbed Zane's arm and nodded to him. After a second's hesitation where he could hear the other man letting out a tremulous breath, Zane nodded back.

They were in agreement. This was it. There was no backing out. Not that Spider would give up this opportunity. Somewhere in his mind he knew he couldn't stop even if he wanted to. Not with the wildness whipping through his body like a chain of firecrackers that, once ignited, couldn't be extinguished. The feeling of being on the cusp of losing control both terrified and thrilled him.

He kept left, making his way along the hall as the music grew louder. He liked the blend of the singer's deep voice and the sad tune. After they were done with the old guy, he'd swipe the CD. And it would be a CD; he was certain. From what he'd seen of Frank, the man was old school so no iTunes for him. Listening to the music later would intensify the memory of what was about to happen. Maybe he'd learn those French lyrics and sing along. It wasn't just accents; he was also pretty good at carrying a tune. Not just pretty good, he corrected himself. He was amazing.

Spider stopped in the doorway to what looked like a lounge room minus a TV. The old man was sitting in a leather armchair under the light of a floor lamp. Spider could only see Frank's face in shadowed profile so he couldn't tell if the man was asleep or listening to the music.

Spider waited a beat hoping the old guy would look his way and see him in the doorway. Absently, he wished for a mask, something freaky to add shock value to what the neighbour would experience in the moment they locked eyes. *Next time.*

Stepping closer, Spider pulled the rope out of the back of his pants. At the same time he flicked the blade open and held it up. This movement got the old man's attention. His bald head swivelled in Spider's direction. Just as Spider had planned, they locked eyes, only there was no trace of surprise or fear in Frank's gaze. What Spider saw was hard and unflinching.

For the first time since planning this little adventure, Spider felt unsure. Unsure of himself and how the situation would go down. It was a fleeting doubt, one that was quickly dismissed. He was younger and stronger than Frank. There were two of them so the odds were in their favour. Again, he was glad he'd brought Zane along. The old guy didn't stand a chance against the two of them, no matter how big he looked or how hard he tried to stare them down.

"How's it going, Frank?" Spider asked, holding the noose up for the man to see. "Feeling blue?"

Behind him, Zane hawked out a laugh that sounded forced and close to hysterical.

Frank's eyes moved to Spider's shoulder. "You the one that pushed her?" he asked Zane. "Did you?" his voice rose. "Did you come into my house and murder my wife?"

"I– I didn't," Zane spluttered.

Spider didn't like this. It wasn't how the moment was supposed to play out. He was meant to be the one doing the talking. He was the one in charge, asking the questions.

"Listen." Spider took a step closer making sure Frank could see the blade. "This could go bad for you so shut the fuck up."

He thought of crouching in front of the man and brandishing the knife in his face, but that look was still in Frank's eyes. A screw you look that Spider didn't care for. Not one bit.

"A little bird told me you have more money hidden in this big house," Spider said, spreading his arms wide so that the noose and blade were clearly on display. "Tell me where it is and we'll leave you to enjoy your music."

The old man took his time looking in Spider's direction. "Spider, is it?" Frank asked. "Bet you came up with that name for yourself, didn't you?"

Spider didn't like the twinkle in the man's eyes when he said his name. Frank was laughing at him, but Spider wouldn't let the old man see he was bothered.

"Don't make me–"

"Your real name is Edward, isn't that right?" Frank baited. "You like pushing women around." He snapped his finger, the dry raspy sound almost making Spider jump. "And posing."

Spider was about to speak when Frank continued. "And you," he said looking to Zane. "You like sponging off women. Pushing old ladies. The pair of you are too dumb to make anything of yourselves so you decided on a life of crime. How original." Frank laughed. "You know what I see? Two skinny little shitheads that have no idea what they're getting themselves into."

"Sh-sh… Shut the f-f fuck–"

Frank laughed. "Stop stuttering, boy. If you come into my house with a knife, you'd better act like a man."

Spider's hands shook and the words that lodged in his throat kept piling up until he thought he'd choke. The only way to smother the shame and the powerlessness he felt was to strike out. And listening to the old man mock him didn't just make Spider angry, it turned his blood to poison, into a thick black tar of hate that he hadn't felt since he found a way to take control of his life. Control of others made him powerful, but right now Frank was in the driver's seat. That was unacceptable.

He used his left hand, the one holding the noose. Swinging back the hand, he hit the old man in a half punch half slap across the mouth. The blow landed with a gratifying *thunk* that rocked Frank's head to the side.

Rather than silencing the old man and putting him back in his place, the assault seemed to amuse him. He turned his face back to Spider and spat. A glob of blood landed at Spider's feet.

"You'll never spend that money. You're going to die here," Frank warned through lips painted red with blood.

"I don't like this," Zane said at Spider's shoulder. "He's crazy."

"Sh-sh shut up," Spider snapped.

Spider wanted to do more than slap Frank, but the old man's death had to look like suicide. He couldn't handle the death of his wife so he hung himself. Easy. A chair, a noose, and a bit of motivation from Spider and his trusty blade. Not just easy, brilliant with a bit of fun thrown in, only Spider wasn't having fun and motivating Frank was anything but easy.

"Let's go," Zane said, getting antsy. "We got the other money. We don't need all this."

The music had stopped and a *tick-tick* replaced the singing. Glancing around, Spider noticed the record player. It briefly registered that he'd been wrong about the CD. He'd been wrong about Frank in any number of ways. But for now, Spider needed to think. There had to be a way to turn this around because he'd slice the old man to pieces before he'd slink away like a beaten dog. That's when he noticed the book on the side table next to Frank's whiskey. A leather book with Amy's name on the cover. It looked expensive. *A special book for a special girl.* Spider felt a spark of pleasure as he realised there was a better way to motivate the old boy.

He waggled the blade near Frank's face. "You're a real dog, Frank. You had the wife and the girl next door on the go at the same time." Spider jerked his chin toward the book. "I bet Amy will be very grateful when she sees that nice book you bought for her. I bet she'll let you put those wrinkly hands all over her tight little body. Or have you already done that?"

There was a change in Frank's expression. It was only a small movement, a tightening of his jaw and movement of his brows. For the first time since they entered the house, Frank looked worried. That's when Spider knew he had him.

"I noticed you still have a landline in the kitchen. That's old school." As Spider talked, Frank's eyes never left his face. That was good. He had the man's undivided attention.

"I think you should call Amy." Spider turned ever so slightly and spoke to Zane. "Tell her something terrible has happened to her favourite older man. There's an ambulance outside Frank's house and that he must be hurt," Spider said in a breathless voice.

"You said we were leaving her out of this," Zane said, sounding confused.

"That's up to Frank," Spider continued.

Now he did risk crouching in front of the old man. "What do you think, mate? Shall we get Amy here? Might be easier if you just tell us where the rest of the money is hidden."

Frank wasn't smiling now. In fact, Spider thought he looked downright scared. The old guy really did have a thing for Amy.

"Guest room." Frank's voice was tight. "Upstairs on the right. It's in the wardrobe, top shelf."

"Go," Spider said to Zane. To Frank, he said, "Good choice. You're a real hard ass. I like that. But this can only go one way." He held the noose up and let it swing back and forth. "As long as you cooperate we'll leave the girl alone."

Watching Frank's eyes as he stared at the noose, Spider felt the return of his earlier excitement. The old man wasn't a pushover and maybe that was a good thing. Just like Spider thought, Frank *was* a learning experience. Too easy was no fun and now things were back on track. His blood was singing.

"You were in the Army?" Spider asked, still crouched in front of the old man. "Is that how you became such a hard man?" Spider was genuinely interested. If things were different, he'd have liked to get to know the man and find out what made him tick.

Frank smiled. It was an unsettling look, revealing blood smeared teeth. Instinctively, Spider pulled back.

"Yes," Frank answered. "By stomping on shitheads like you."

Spider forced a laugh, hating that the man was still getting to him. It helped knowing that within twenty minutes Frank would be dangling from the end of a rope. Still, Spider considered driving his elbow into Frank's chest. Not hard enough to bruise his old skin, but with just enough force to wipe the smile off his face.

"Shit, Spider?" Zane called from the hall. "I can't find the light switch." This was followed by a crash and a clatter of breaking china.

Spider stood and backed towards the door, careful to keep his eyes on the old man in the chair.

"Zane!" Spider hissed. "Stop wrecking the place and get in here."

Zane arrived a second later looking red faced and breathless. "This place is huge. I can't see the stairs in the dark."

Spider, still watching Frank, handed Zane the knife. "Watch him and don't let him move until I get back." He put some exasperation into his voice, but in truth he was glad for a reason to get away from the old man's death stare.

He shoved the noose down the back of his jeans and spoke to Frank. "Try anything and I'll gut Amy like a sow."

Feeling like he'd sufficiently warned the man, Spider plodded down the hall. As he walked, he trailed his hand along the wall, feeling for a switch. Zane was right. The house was huge. He'd been in this part of the house less than a week ago, but somehow the place seemed bigger in the dark. As he edged further away from the room where Frank listened to records, the rest of the house sat in almost total blackness.

He was just about to pull out his phone when his fingers found the switch. Marvelling at how inept Zane was at even the simplest of tasks, Spider flicked the switch. Nothing happened so he tried clicking it back and forth. Zilch.

"Christ." Spider snatched his phone out of his pocket and turned on its light. Almost immediately, blue light landed on an upturned hallstand and a scatter of fragmented china. It wouldn't do to have the cops wondering why a suicidal man would stop to break some china. The mess would have to be cleaned up before they left. A job for Zane, Spider decided. *You break it, you clear it.*

He turned to his left and spotted the stairs. Before climbing, he called out to Zane. "All okay in there?"

"All good," came Zane's reply.

At least there was something he could cope with on his own. Spider just hoped he could keep the old man under control for a few minutes. Everything about this night had been weird, he thought, heading up the stairs. It started out better than okay with the open gate, the outside light left on and then the back door sitting unlocked. After that things had gone sideways.

Spider was a few steps up and still holding the phone for light when he stopped suddenly. Thinking back to the moment he'd seen the side gate propped open, he remembered thinking Frank must be going senile because he'd made it too easy to enter the property.

"Too easy," Spider muttered.

Only Frank was far from confused. The gate, the light, and the unlocked door weren't mistakes. Spider frowned. What was it he'd thought when he'd seen the open gate? *An open gate invited visitors.* Standing on the darkened staircase, he felt his stomach shrivel. They weren't hunting Frank Foxhall. Instead, Frank had laid a trap and they'd fallen into it.

He was about to turn and run when the phone beeped in his hand. A message from Zane. Spider was about to call out to Zane when he saw it was more than a message. A picture had been attached. He noticed the little white sideways arrow and realised it wasn't a picture, but a clip.

Spider touched the arrow and instantly recognised two things: the crappy 80s draining board and the wad of cash. When the flame touched the money, his eyes grew wide, first in disbelief and then in horror. His money was literally going up in smoke.

His first thought was Zane. How was he doing this and why? His hand tightened around the mobile as he read the message that wasn't a message at all and more of a calling card. *Splat.* He felt like the flames had jumped off the screen and into his brain, burning him with scalding anger.

Splat the freak. Splat the scared little mouse who jumped every time he entered the room. *She* was taunting *him?* It was beyond comprehension that she would have the nerve to take what was his. To take *his* money.

In that moment he knew he was going to kill her. Zane, Frank, none of them mattered. Spider wouldn't need a blade or a noose, just his hands. He wanted to feel her death skin on skin.

Still on the stairs, he hit play again wanting to watch the moment when Splat signed her own death warrant. Needing to watch the money burn so that it could fuel his rage, so engrossed in what he was seeing and feeling he barely noticed taking another step up the stairs.

His boot caught on something and he tripped. If he hadn't been holding the phone, he might have had time to put his hand out and catch himself before he hit the stair.

He landed hard, the right side of his face slamming down on what felt like a million spikes. In the dark, he couldn't see the plank of timber and rows of curved and rusty six-inch nails sticking up like evil teeth. At the same time his left elbow seemed to rip in two. A scream filled his head. The world wavered into grey and then snapped back to agony. Panicked, he tried to stand. As he did, the pain intensified and for a sickening moment it felt like his face was being ripped off his bones.

Chapter Thirty-four

Spider's slap had knocked Frank's head sideways and both men's faces swam before his eyes. For a second or two the world greyed, but then came back into focus. With the taste of blood on his tongue, he managed to arrange his features into a smile.

Spider was clearly the one in charge. A sociopath and a narcissist. Frank had come across his type before. In Vietnam he'd learned how dangerous and sadistic men like Spider could be. Frank also knew their sense of superiority left them open to manipulation.

The other one, Zane, was the eager lapdog, edgy and unpredictable. Together they were capable of anything, but right now Frank's priority was getting Zane alone. As it turned out that's just how it happened.

Once Spider left the room, Frank went to work on the other one. "Does he always tell you what to do?" he asked. "Did he tell you to kill my wife?"

"Shut up," Zane whispered.

Not to be put off, Frank continued. "Do you think he's going to stick around once he's got the money?"

They could hear Spider moving around in the hall. Frank watched Zane glance towards the sounds they both heard. *He doesn't like being alone with me.*

"I bet this was his idea wasn't it?" Frank asked. When Zane didn't answer, he continued. "I reckon your friend has an exit plan. And sure as God made little green apples, you're not part of it."

Zane looked about ready to tell Frank to shut up again when a scream tore through the air – a scream that told Frank all he needed to know.

Zane turned towards the sound giving Frank the opportunity to grab the hammer he'd hidden on the far side of the armchair. Zane might have caught Frank's movement out of the corner of his eyes or maybe he just hesitated. It didn't matter because when Zane looked back, Frank was already raising his weapon.

To Frank's surprise, Zane didn't hesitate. He swung the knife. The blade caught Frank across his left upper arm, tearing through his shirt and slicing flesh. Zane was drawing back for another assault, aiming higher this time, when Frank made his move.

His reflexes were still fast – fast enough to grab Zane's wrist in mid-air. Once Frank had hold of the arm wielding the knife, he forced it down and pinned Zane's hand to the arm of the chair. At the same time he swung the hammer.

Seeing the blow coming, Zane shrieked and lifted his shoulder in an exaggerated shrug then twisted his upper body away so that when the head of the hammer hit it missed his skull and slammed against his shoulder. There was an audible crunch, like the sound of a dry branch snapping in a storm. Zane screamed, his cry almost matching the ones that were coming from the stairs.

Frank was on his feet now. Zane's shoulder hung in an unnatural slope. His knees had buckled and the young man had hit the floor. Standing over him, Frank raised the hammer.

The young man who murdered Greta in her own home was sobbing, his mouth open with snot covering his lips. "Please, don't." Zane shuffled on his knees trying to crawl away. "I'm sorry. Please, I'm hurt real bad. I'll give the money back."

Frank's mind went to his last moments with Greta, and the fear and confusion in her eyes as she repeated the words: *Who are you? What are you doing here?* Had the young man shown her any mercy? He'd promised himself and Greta that there would be justice, yet he couldn't bring himself to swing the hammer one final time.

What he could see in his future was regret, perhaps for only hours or stretching out over the last days of his life. The arm holding the hammer was tiring, but Frank made no move to strike. The snivelling coward on the floor would be easy to dispatch. One solid hit and it would be over. God, how Frank wanted it all to be over.

If he caved the young man's head in, would it change anything? Would it bring him peace? Frank gritted his teeth trying to see the man not as a weeping dastard, but as the thug that stole Greta's life. The animal that put his hands on the kindest person Frank had ever known.

"Don't hurt me, please," Zane begged, shuffling closer to the armchair.

The pain came like a bullet in the chest, rocking Frank on his heels. Stabbing and constricting pain that engulfed his upper body and snatched the breath from his lungs. It lasted only seconds, but long enough for his arm to quiver and lose strength.

With his free hand, he clutched his chest trying to massage away the pain. "Not now," he gasped.

Zane swivelled back towards Frank, the knife still in hand. As the tidal wave of pain that had gripped Frank's heart lessened, Zane stabbed the blade deep into Frank's thigh.

Frank felt the knife like a clout and with more surprise than pain. His legs buckled and as he sank, Frank took in

Zane's face. Bared teeth and crazed eyes. Any fragment of pity or hesitation he had for the young man vanished.

Without forethought, Frank slammed the hammer down on Zane's head with all the force he could muster, the kind of force that was depleted but still enough to thump the left side of Zane's skull with a solid *crack*. Zane's head seemed to bounce on his neck before his entire body slumped sideways.

Every remnant of strength left Frank's body and he sunk beside Zane. Frank felt no satisfaction, no sense of relief; only cold creeping into his bones and numbness of mind. A numbness that was as welcome as the slowing of his heart. He didn't know if Zane was alive or dead nor did he care. The concerns that had burned brightly only hours ago now faded as his breathing grew shallow.

Chapter Thirty-five

Amy stashed the phone in her pocket and headed for the front door. No point going out the bathroom window when no one was home. Just as she was about to pull the door closed behind her, she heard a scream. The sound was somehow heightened by the darkness.

Amy let go of the door. Another shriek, this one was less ear-splitting but still echoed with pain. The screams were coming from the Foxhalls' house. They were in his house. She didn't bother with the stairs and jumped onto the path. Her only thought was Frank.

Running, she pictured Greta's body on the kitchen floor and the halo of blood surrounding her head. Amy's feet were moving fast, too fast. In the dark she didn't see Spider's Holden until she was almost on top of it. When she put on the brakes, momentum flung her into the car.

She hit the vehicle with a thump and came to a stop. The shock of the impact gave her a few seconds for her mind to catch up with her movements. What was she doing? If Zane and Spider were in Frank's house, how could she stop them? By rushing in, could she save Frank or only make things worse?

She had to make a decision, one that would have consequences. But hadn't she always known it would come to this? Without hesitating, she pulled out her phone and Worsten's card. With shaking fingers, she misdialled the first time. On the second go she managed to make the call. On the other end, the phone rang four times then went to messages.

"Damn, damn, damn." She was still repeating the word when the beep sounded for her to leave a message. "I need help. Something's happening at Frank's house. Frank Foxhall. He's in danger." Amy realised she wasn't making any sense so she tried again. "This is Amy Holt. There are two men in Frank's house. I think they're going to kill him."

It wasn't enough. Frank needed help now. This time she rang triple zero and told the operator that her neighbour was being attacked. She gave the address, but when the dispatcher told her to stay on the line she hung up.

There came another cry, not as loud as the others. Or it could have come from a bird startled into blind flight. Amy dragged her fingers through her hair. She couldn't just stand and wait. By the time the police arrived Frank might be dead. *He might be dead now – dead just like Greta and Travis.* That last cry had been weak. No, she wouldn't believe that. Frank was strong. He was alive.

Why had she told Zane and Spider there was more money? She should have known the two men wouldn't be able to resist going back to her neighbour's house looking for more cash. That was it. Amy pushed off the Holden and started jogging next door. Money was the key that just might buy Frank a bit more time.

The front of the house was dark and there were no more cries. There was no sound at all. Somehow that was worse than the screams. Amy stepped up onto the veranda. Under the circumstances, the idea of knocking seemed ludicrous. Instead, she tried the doorknob. Frank said he was going to lock up yet the lever turned in her hand and the door swung in.

Save a small pool of light spilling out of the sitting room, the home's interior sat in darkness. A dense kind of blackness that seemed impossible even at night. She'd been in the Foxhalls' at night and on those occasions lights were burning and the rooms were filled with delicious smells. Tonight she felt claustrophobic: shuttered and caged.

Amy forced her feet to keep moving towards the distant puddle of light. She didn't want to linger or think about what might be hidden in the dark. *Not what, but who.*

"Frank?" She called his name, startled by how frightened she sounded.

In response, she heard groaning and more disturbing movement off to her right. Was it breathing or just the sound of her shoes scuffing the floor? Nothing she saw or heard seemed right, so she hurried on.

Unprepared for what she found in the sitting room, she let out a yelp and covered her mouth. Blood. Two bodies on the floor. Frank slumped over Zane's legs. Both men gory messes. The horror immobilized her so all she could do was stare.

"Frank?" she whispered.

His mouth opened and choked on a breath. He was alive. Amy rushed closer and dropped to her knees, touching a hand to his chest. There was movement beneath her palm, the rise and fall of his breathing.

"It's okay. I'm here," she said, searching for the source of a wound.

She found two wounds, one on his arm and the other on his thigh. He was losing blood too rapidly from his leg. She scanned the room searching for something to put on the wound and stem the bleeding.

It was then she realised Zane was also breathing, shallow rasping breaths that sounded like hiccupping sobs. But rather than go to his aid she concentrated on Frank.

With nothing else available, she grabbed the throw rug off the sofa, wadded it up and pressed it to Frank's thigh. Using her left hand to keep the pad in place, she pulled out her phone with her free hand and made another triple zero call.

This time she asked for an ambulance. The dispatcher, a woman, asked questions. "Is he breathing? Is he conscious?" Amy did her best to answer and follow instructions, but her limbs were shaking and the dispatcher's words seemed like a foreign language.

"Weapon?" Amy caught the last word of the dispatcher's question.

Weapon? Amy looked around and spotted a hammer near Frank's leg and a knife still cradled in Zane's hand. Both items were bloody.

"Yes," Amy said gripping the phone. "A hammer and a knife. Please, I need help. I need an ambulance."

She put the phone on speaker and set it on the floor while still holding the makeshift wad to Frank's thigh. How long had it been since she'd called the police? Ten minutes? Fifteen? Zane was making gurgling sounds and Amy noticed blood oozing out of his ear.

"I don't know what to do." She had no idea who she was speaking to: herself, the dispatcher, Frank or even Zane.

All she knew was both men were badly injured and perhaps near death. She was alone and so far out of her depth it felt like she was drowning. At the same time, she could feel blood soaking through the knees of her jeans.

"An ambulance is on its way. You're doing well." The dispatcher's disembodied voice came from the phone.

Doing well? The words didn't compute. Amy used her free hand to take hold of Frank's. His skin felt cold, much colder than the blood soaking her clothes.

"Don't die, Frank," she said leaning close to his ear. "The ambulance is coming so try and hang on. Please."

His lids fluttered. "Greta?"

For a second, she thought of saying yes she was Greta. Would it hurt to give him what he wanted? In the end, she couldn't bring herself to deceive him.

"It's Amy. You're going to be okay. Just stay awake."

Frank opened his eyes. "I'm dying. Let me go, Amy."

She opened her mouth to tell him to hang on, but a hand snatched hold of her hair and yanked her backwards. She was pulled off her knees and onto her butt. Her scalp lifted and burned as she was dragged across the floor. In spite of the shock and pain, all she could think of was the wad of blanket and how she had let it go.

The pulling stopped and a face loomed over her. A face so mangled, it took her seconds before she recognised Spider.

"You fucking bitch." His words were slushy as blood spilled from the shredded mess that was now his mouth. "You planned this," he said.

A chunk of flesh was missing from his upper lip so as he spoke his gums and teeth were visible. His left eye was little more than a dark hole filled with what looked like blackcurrant jam. Amy shrieked and tried to pull away, wanting to escape the skeleton-like mouth and the grizzly eye. At the same time her mind was struggling to understand what she was seeing.

"You told me there was more money. You set me up." He leaned in so that his vile lips were only inches above hers. "You burnt my money, but you're not laughing now, are you?"

"I didn't. I promise!" Amy forced herself to think. "I only burned the one roll. I was angry. I'm sorry. There's at least ninety thousand left. Just take it and go."

Spider's remaining eye shifted off her face and scanned the room. Either he was thinking or searching for something. When he looked back, his lips were drawn back in what she realised was a smile. His weight shifted off her as he pulled her around.

"Are you watching old man?" Spider yelled over his shoulder.

Amy let her head drop to the side. She could see Frank. His eyes were open and one hand was clamped to his chest. Spider's hands clamped around her throat and squeezed. The pain ripped through her throat and the air in her lungs turned cold.

She grabbed at Spider's arms, trying to tear him off her. The cold in her chest turned into heat as she struggled for air. Spider was screaming at her, but she couldn't hear the words over the buzzing in her head. Her face was still turned towards Frank and her neck was pinned in place.

The panic exploding inside her was ebbing as Spider's fingers squeezed. Amy took in the world in fading snaps. The armchair, Zane's body and, finally, Frank motioning with his thumb. Was he giving her a thumbs up as she died? Her oxygen-starved brain tried to make sense of what she was seeing.

Spider may have loosened his fingers or she might have stopped struggling long enough for her mind to begin working again, either way she suddenly knew exactly what Frank was trying to tell her.

With her neck pinned in place, she could only turn her head slightly as she pulled at his forearms. She rolled her eyes in Spider's direction. His one eye sparkled and he leaned closer possibly enjoying these last moments or relishing watching her terrified gaze.

Amy let go of Spider and snaked her right hand up between his arms. She curled her fingers into a fist and jammed her thumb into his injured eye. Not sure if she had the power to make the attack count, she shoved with what was left of her strength. As she shoved she turned her thumb, corkscrewing it into the bloody socket.

Spider howled and let go of her neck. Amy sucked in air that came only in whips over damaged tissue. Above her Spider screamed, fell to the side, and clamped his hands to his face.

"Run. Run." She heard the words, but couldn't be sure if they were coming from Frank or just bouncing around inside her brain.

Running seemed impossible when her lungs were still struggling to draw breath. The closest she could come to moving was to roll onto her side. Coughing and wheezing, spots danced across her vision and water streamed from her eyes.

"Run." This time she was sure it was Frank's voice urging her to escape.

Gagging now, Amy scrambled onto her hands and knees and shuffled forward. The hall was still in total darkness so she had no way of being sure she was even heading in the right direction.

"I'm going to kill you." Spider was screaming threats, but she couldn't tell if he'd given chase.

Still crawling, Amy picked up speed and didn't dare look back. Two or three more shuffles and she risked standing. On shaky legs, she stumbled forward, arms held straight out searching for the door. Behind her she heard a scuffle and this time she did look back.

In the pool of light emanating from the study, she could see Spider and Frank. The younger man still had a hand clamped to his face and Frank was half draped, half falling over Spider's shoulder.

"Go," Frank said in a voice barely loud enough to carry the length of the hall.

Amy turned away, her watering eyes now producing real tears. She pushed forward a few more staggering steps when her hand hit something solid. With her palms flat she felt the door until her fingers found the knob. She heard a thump behind her but didn't stop. The knob turned and she found herself outside.

There was moonlight and blessedly cool night air. She managed to stay on her feet as she hit the steps. More lights, blue and red, and a voice before a figure emerged.

For a horrifying second she thought Spider had somehow appeared in front of her.

"Stop! Get on the ground."

She didn't recognise the man at first, but something about his voice sparked a memory. Worsten! In the light of the police cars she saw the detective and took another shaky step.

She opened her mouth, but her throat produced only a croak. Worsten grabbed her and pulled her to his side just as her legs wobbled and almost gave out. He was still shouting, but not looking at Amy. His right arm was out in front of him and Amy realised he was holding a gun.

Spider came down the veranda at full speed and then seemed to try to back step. Amy heard other voices and car doors slamming.

"Police! Get on the ground!" Worsten's voice boomed louder than the others.

It didn't matter that she was held by an armed officer, when she saw Spider, she wanted to run.

Spider stood motionless for a moment, still clutching his eye. "I'm hurt," he said in a high-pitched voice. "I need help."

Worsten continued to order him to get on the ground. To Amy's surprise, Spider obeyed and crumpled on top of the lawn. Two uniformed officers rushed him, their backs blocking him from view.

Chapter Thirty-six

Amy sat in the back of Worsten's car with the door open, watching as ambulances filled the lane. The rescue vehicles came one after another making her wonder if every ambulance in Bunbury was now on Cobblestone Lane. It was a silly thought, but what else was there to do but wait and wonder until a stretcher carried Frank out of the house? Zane had already been trundled along the path and into one of the rescue vehicles.

Worsten was in the house while Amy wondered if Frank was alive or dead. At times her mind would jump from thinking about Frank and replay the moment when she'd thought she was going to die at Spider's hands. During all this, she tried not to rest her hands on her jeans that were still damp with blood. Asking questions was out because her throat was so swollen she could barely swallow.

Spider was somewhere, in an ambulance or a police car. She'd lost track of the comings and goings. One thing she was determined to do was keep her eyes trained on the front of the Foxhalls' house. Keeping her eyes on the door also meant not having to look at her bloody hands.

Time passed. She didn't know how much. The night air turned colder, chilling her arms and face. Finally, a stretcher wheeled out of the front door and down the steps. Amy scrambled out of the car, but was stopped by the outstretched arm of a young cop.

"You'll have to wait here," he said, blocking her view.

She didn't bother trying to argue because the effort of producing sound was beyond her ability. Instead, she simply sidestepped and watched as Frank was carried to an ambulance.

At first she could see only blankets, but finally she caught a glimpse of Frank's face obscured by an oxygen mask. He was alive. If she had a voice, she'd have called to him. *I'm here!* She heard the words clearly in her mind.

As the stretcher came closer, Amy dodged the cop and rushed forward. Just for a second, Frank's eyes opened and looked her way. She reached out a hand to touch him, but his fingers were out of reach. A few seconds later he was ensconced in the ambulance.

* * *

The never-ending night stretched on and on. At Worsten's insistence she was taken to hospital where her clothes were bagged and taken as evidence. Then she was examined and photographed, the camera taking in every shameful bruise of the last few days' abuse. Mercifully, her attending doctor declared her unable to answer questions. At some point in the early hours she was allowed to sleep.

The following afternoon Worsten appeared in her room. "You look better," he said, pulling up a chair.

Amy nodded, not really believing that she looked anything close to better. An earlier glimpse in the mirror at her bruised and swollen neck together with the burst blood vessels in her eyes had told a different story.

"Your boyfriend and his friend Edward Crease have both been transferred to Royal Perth Hospital. You're safe here," he said.

She hadn't thought of the detective as kind, but there was compassion in his voice.

"I wanted to be the one to tell you," he hesitated. "Frank passed away last night."

Amy found herself staring at the detective's mouth, trying to make sense of what he was saying. Frank couldn't be dead. He was alive when they put him in the ambulance so he couldn't have bled to death. He'd saved her from Spider. Didn't that prove he was still strong?

"He was a very sick man and with everything that his body went through..." Worsten shrugged. "The doctors think he had a heart attack."

Sick? Amy grimaced and shook her head. Greta was sick, but Frank was robust.

Misunderstanding her reaction, Worsten continued. "Don't blame yourself. You did everything you could to save him. You did well keeping him alive until help arrived."

She couldn't stand much more. Frustration and grief welled up until all she could do was drop her face in her hands and sob. Worsten tried to say something comforting, but in the end he gave up and went to find a nurse. In the midst of a busy hospital with people bustling around outside her door, Amy felt like the loneliest person in the world.

* * *

"Before we start, I want it to be clear that you've asked to make a voluntary statement and you have chosen to do so without having a solicitor present. Is that correct?" Worsten asked.

When Amy nodded, he asked her to answer for the recording.

"Yes," Amy replied.

They were in an interview room at the Bunbury Police Station five days after the night Frank died and Spider tried to strangle her. Her voice was still hoarse and talking was painful, but she was determined to tell her story and accept the consequences, whatever they might be.

"Okay. Could you start by telling me about the night Frank Foxhall died?" Worsten asked.

There was a paper cup filled with water on the table between them. Amy took a sip before she began.

"It didn't start that night," she said, setting the cup down. "About a week ago I found some money in a bag under Frank's and Greta's bed. I mentioned the money to my boyfriend, Zane Bryson." Amy touched a hand to her neck where the skin was still puffy and bruised.

"No, that's not right either." She shook her head and pulled out her phone, showing Worsten the photograph of Travis. "It started about ten months ago. There was a young man named Travis," she continued.

She caught the look of confusion in the detective's eyes. She was jumping backwards, but if she was going to tell her story in a way that made sense, she had to go further back. Back to the beginning so she could confess to the act that weighed most heavily on her conscience.

She talked for almost an hour stopping only to take breaks when her voice waned. During those intervals, she'd take small, measured sips of water. When she continued, she told Worsten everything that happened between her, Zane, Spider and the Foxhalls. There was so much to tell that at times the words were tumbling out. It might have been her imagination, but it seemed some of the darkness that had flanked her for so long had started to lift.

All that was missing from her story were the details about the real Frank Foxhall, and how the Frank that Amy knew had assumed his identity. Those were not her secrets. They were Frank's and she intended to keep them always.

"Did Frank ever tell you why he kept such a large sum of money in the house?" Worsten asked.

Amy answered without hesitation. "No, but Frank and Greta were rich so I thought that maybe that's what rich people did."

It was half true and to her relief Worsten seemed satisfied with the answer. He asked a few more questions about her reasons for not reporting Zane and Spider to the police after what they did to Greta. This time Amy answered with as much honesty and accuracy as she could remember.

When he turned off the tape, Worsten stayed seated and Amy had the impression that he had something on his mind – something he didn't want recorded.

"The day Frank died, he visited his solicitor. Did you know about that?" He raised his eyebrows waiting for her to answer.

Amy shook her head, but said nothing. Her throat was burning from the effort of so much talking and she had no idea where he was headed.

"Frank gave his solicitor, a man named Andrew March, a letter and instructions to forward to me when he passed away." He paused, maybe waiting for her to comment. When she didn't, he continued. "It wasn't a letter really, but a written confession. Frank confessed to the murder of his brother Ron. He gave details that contributed weight to his confession, but…" Worsten held up his index finger "… he said nothing about his motive. Nothing about why he would plan and execute a murder. So, Amy…" Worsten pinned her with his gaze. "Do you have any idea why Frank murdered his brother?"

Amy was careful to stare into the detective's eyes when she answered. "I have no idea."

Chapter Thirty-seven

A month is a long time or, depending on how one judged it, no time at all. In the four weeks since Amy had been back in Perth and home with her mother and sister, time held little meaning. Her body had mostly healed, but her mind was still on Cobblestone Lane.

Not yet ready to look for work, she'd taken to daily walks. Short but hurried journeys around the block had turned into hour-long stints where she took long purposeful strides while her mind worked over the days she'd spent in Bunbury. Replaying horrors, examining actions, and reliving them – always reliving them.

Much of the time, her footfalls matched her constant mantra; *I won't see him today*. But she always did. Spider driving a passing car, a blond-haired jogger rounding the corner or a man in a tight T-shirt stepping off a bus. Always harmless strangers, but his face was constantly there. When she didn't see him at every turn, Spider was waiting in her dreams where she was forced to look at his ruined face. *I won't see him today. I won't see him today*. After three weeks, he stopped appearing: mostly.

During one of these marches with Spider nowhere in sight, Amy realised she was thinking less about the devastating end to her time on Cobblestone Lane and more about the days she'd spent getting to know Frank and Greta. Glimpses of happiness, or at the very least memories of that feeling. It was progress, she told herself each day as she pulled off her winter coat and sank exhausted onto the sofa. She didn't bother trying to fool herself into believing she was completely whole again, but it was getting easier to look at her own reflection. Easier to look at her hands without imagining them coated with blood.

The key, she'd learned, was not to overthink things. If the sky was cloudy and the roads shiny after a shower, it was better to savour the smell of streets washed clean by the autumn rain and the touch of the wind blowing her hair back so her face felt pleasantly cool. Stay in the moment for as long as possible. More than exercising, she was cleansing herself of the corrupt life she'd lived with Zane. Ridding herself of Zane while he was still in a rehabilitation hospital recovering from a brain injury that would most likely leave him permanently disabled.

It was on her return from one of her soul-cleansing marches with her face tingling from the sting of the gust and her teeth cold against her lips, as she grappled with her coming sentencing date and what life might be like for a single twenty-eight-year-old with a criminal record, that she noticed an unfamiliar car parked on the street outside her mother's house. Not the dark sedan she associated with Worsten's visits. There had been a few of those, but not lately. This vehicle was something different, a BMW, sleek and expensive-looking.

Her stomach flip-flopped with trepidation. Reminding herself that Spider was still in custody and she had nothing left to hide didn't dispel the feeling that something was wrong. The flashy silver car looked incongruent in front of the unremarkable brick and tile bungalow. *I won't see him today*. But one day soon she'd have to face him when she gave testimony at his trial. The owner of the silver car wasn't Spider, but she guessed he was the reason for the visit.

When she entered the house, her mother met her at the door.

"There's a man here to see you." Catherine seemed uncharacteristically flustered. "Andrew March, a solicitor. He wouldn't say what it's about." She indicated to the lounge room.

Amy frowned trying to place the familiar name.

"Do you want me to come in with you?"

There was a look in her mother's eyes; one Amy was all too familiar with. A look that spoke of sleepless nights of worry and a growing feeling that she no longer really knew her own daughter. There were many sins competing for pieces of Amy's soul, but none worse than knowing she'd put that look on her mother's face.

"No, I'll see him alone," Amy replied.

When Catherine looked uncertain, Amy took her mother's hand and gave it a gentle squeeze. "It's nothing to worry about, promise."

Her mother still looked unconvinced. Not that Amy could blame her. How many promises and platitudes had she heard from her daughter over the last year? How many lies?

Catherine held fast to her daughter's hand for another second. "I'll be in the kitchen if you need me."

Andrew March stood when Amy entered the room, his smile warm and his hand outstretched. In a dark suit and crisp white shirt, he looked nothing like Amy's court appointed legal aid with her messy bun, voluminous satchel filled with files, and harried eyes. How, Amy wondered, was Spider affording this level of representation.

"Miss Holt," he said taking her hand. "I'm Andrew March. I'm very happy to meet you."

She allowed him to shake her hand, if a brief touch could be considered a shake. It occurred to her that

Spider's solicitor shouldn't be talking to her, but she wasn't sure if that was how things worked. The words *conflict of interest* came to mind, but did they fit the situation? Could she refuse to speak to this elegant-looking man? Was elegant a word used to describe a man's appearance? Amy stopped her mental rambling when Andrew March sat and opened his briefcase.

"I don't know if I should be speaking to you," she said, still standing. "I'm a witness for the prosecution and you're..." She waved a hand. "You know."

He set down the papers he pulled out. "Sorry. I probably didn't make myself clear. I'm here on Frank Foxhall's behalf. I was his solicitor and the executor of his estate."

"I thought you were…" She stopped. With the wind taken out of her, she sat in the armchair with furrowed brows. "You're here about Frank?"

"Yes, that's right." Andrew lifted the open briefcase from the sofa and set it on the coffee table. "I would have been in touch sooner, but the circumstances were a bit unusual, what with Frank's death coming so soon after his wife's."

His wife. Amy was trying to keep up with the solicitor, but so far she had no idea what was going on. Possibly picking up on her confusion, he gave a wry smile.

"You see, when Greta Foxhall died she left her entire estate to her husband, Frank, but before her will could go through the usual probate process Frank also passed away." The solicitor spread his hands wide in a *so-you-see* gesture.

Amy nodded. She understood what he was telling her, but still didn't see what any of it had to do with her.

"On the day he died Frank made a new will leaving the bulk of his estate to you."

"Oh." It was all she could muster.

"It's a fairly substantial amount," the solicitor continued, picking up a sheaf of papers. "Um… The family home on Cobblestone Lane, an amount of money – thirty-two-thousand dollars and change – in a savings account." He looked up and pushed his wire-rimmed spectacles up the bridge of his nose. "I believe there is a sum of money held by the police as evidence. Eighty-two thousand, I'm told. I've already started the process of having those funds returned to the estate. There's also a parcel of land." He regarded his paperwork. "A ten-hectare vacant lot abutting the Foxhalls' home. It was Frank's wish that you would keep the lot as bushland to protect the native flora and fauna. Of course, once the property is yours, you can do what you like with it. Finally," he said letting out a breath, "there are two other properties on Cobblestone Lane, but Frank has instructed me to sell those homes and donate the money to a charity that provides money for the care of burn victims."

Amy shook her head trying to process what she was hearing. Frank had left her the house and a large amount of money. It was impossible. While she cared deeply for Greta and Frank, maybe even loved them, this was too much.

"I can't," she said when she finally found her voice. "It's too much. They only knew me for a few months and things…" She wrung her hands together. "Well, they didn't end well. I can't take their money. I don't deserve it."

Andrew put the papers down and fixed her with his light brown eyes that, behind the spectacles, looked like pebbles washed clean by rushing water. They were sensitive eyes, but also knowing. She couldn't help wondering how much he knew about the Foxhalls, or at least suspected.

"These are Frank's wishes," he said gently. "On the day he came to see me, he said you might react this way. That's why Frank insisted I see you in person and not deliver the news over the phone. He also said that he and Greta had grown very fond of you and that your kindness meant a great deal to them." He tapped the papers. "Frank believed in you and he wanted you to have the opportunity to do something with your life. This was his way of giving you that opportunity."

Suddenly, all she could think about was how much she missed Frank and Greta and how she'd never hear Greta play the piano again or chat with Frank as he drove her to work. The loss of the two people that gave her so much more than friendship was overwhelming.

The more she tried to hold back the tears the harder she cried. With her face in her hands, she didn't so much breakdown as crumple. Her reaction sent the solicitor out of the room in search of her mother.

True to form, Catherine took control of the situation and moved the meeting into the kitchen where she made strong cups of tea and set a box of tissue in front of her daughter. She then sat with her arm around Amy as Andrew recounted the details of Frank's will.

Catherine asked a series of questions – sensible questions that Amy would never have thought to ask. While she listened to her mother's voice some semblance of calm returned. Could she do this? Could she accept the Foxhalls' money and, as Frank said, do something with her life? With the tears shed, she felt a spark of something she'd thought she'd lost on Cobblestone Lane: hope.

"I expect probate will take between four to six weeks. I'll keep you updated as the process nears its completion." Before he closed his briefcase, Andrew March pulled out a business card. "I've been following your case on the news and I believe you have a sentencing date coming up."

As she did any time the charges against her were mentioned, Amy felt a flood of shame. She sensed her mother's body stiffening next to her, so she placed a hand on her mother's knee to prevent Catherine from rushing to her defence.

"That's right," Amy said, forcing herself to stare the solicitor in the eyes. "I was charged with unlawful disposal of a corpse. I've pleaded guilty to the charge."

What she didn't say was that Worsten had gone easy on her. Taking her confession and willingness to testify against Spider into consideration, the detective had decided not to include failing to render aid and assistance and failure to report a death to the charges and, as her legal aid had reminded her on more than one occasion, when it came to Greta's death, Detective Worsten could have made a case for accessory to murder.

Andrew nodded. "I've made a call to a colleague of mine named Anton Seaber. He's a very skilled criminal solicitor, not cheap, but under the circumstances you can afford him." He held the card out for Amy to take. "Having someone like Anton in your corner will mean the difference between a custodial or suspended sentence. He's waiting for your call."

"Why are you helping me like this?" Amy asked making no move to take the card. "You must know what I've done?"

"Yes, I know you were involved in what happened to Greta, but I also know that involvement doesn't mean guilt." He put the card on the table and slid it towards Amy. "I didn't know Frank well, but I did know Greta. She was an exceptional woman and I trust her judgement. Frank told me she judged you to be a kind young woman with a promising future."

Catherine saw the solicitor to the door. When she returned, Amy was holding the business card Andrew had left for her.

"Well?" her mother asked.

Amy hesitated. What Frank had done for her would change her life and the lives of her mother and sister. For the first time in her life she allowed herself to consider a future that included university, travel, and a worthwhile occupation. Yet, she wanted to face up to the things she'd done. Greta and Travis deserved justice. If she didn't give them that, could she ever move forward with her life? But did justice mean suffering? Prison would change her, probably not for the better. Was there a chance she could be judged for her crimes without sacrificing her future to them?

"I'll make the call," she said.

The End

If you enjoyed this book, please let others know by leaving a quick review on Amazon. Also, if you spot anything untoward in the paperback, get in touch. We strive for the best quality and appreciate reader feedback.

editor@thebookfolks.com

www.thebookfolks.com

Also by Anna Willett

BACKWOODS RIPPER
RETRIBUTION RIDGE
UNWELCOME GUESTS
FORGOTTEN CRIMES
CRUELTY'S DAUGHTER
VENGEANCE BLIND
THE WOMAN BEHIND HER

SMALL TOWN NIGHTMARE
COLD VALLEY NIGHTMARE
SAVAGE BAY NIGHTMARE

PEST
BEAST

FREE with Kindle Unlimited and available in paperback from Amazon.

Made in the USA
Middletown, DE
19 February 2021